He hadn't known she was pregnant...

He'd never have sent her away if he had. But he'd done it for her own good, so she could have the career in the city that she'd always wanted. He stared up at Abby's apartment. He could only imagine the fears she must be facing now. Was she sleeping? Holding Robbie in her arms? Crying her eyes out?

Nick had to stop feeling sorry for her. She should have told him he was a father—come back to him so they could raise the boy together.

In his mind's eye he saw her when she'd opened the door to him earlier, looking as beautiful as he'd remembered. But now she had the curves of a woman. The urge to touch her, to feel her against him, had assailed him, taking all his willpower to withstand it. He'd had to tuck his hands into the back pockets of his jeans so she wouldn't notice the shaking.

But he had to resist her.

He'd come for his son.

Judy Christenberry

has written over seventy books
for Silhouette Books®, and she's a favorite
with readers. Now you can find Judy's books
in the Harlequin Romance® and
American Romance® lines!

Step into a world where family counts,
men are true to their word—
and where romance always wins the day!

*No one writes Christmas like Judy,
so don't miss her festive duet
Mistletoe & Marriage*

*November: The Cowboy's Christmas Proposal
December: Snowbound with Mr. Right*

JUDY CHRISTENBERRY

The Cowboy's Secret Son

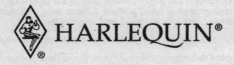

HARLEQUIN®

TORONTO • NEW YORK • LONDON
AMSTERDAM • PARIS • SYDNEY • HAMBURG
STOCKHOLM • ATHENS • TOKYO • MILAN • MADRID
PRAGUE • WARSAW • BUDAPEST • AUCKLAND

ISBN-13: 978-0-373-03961-6
ISBN-10:   0-373-03961-1

THE COWBOY'S SECRET SON

First North American Publication 2007.

Judy Christenberry has been writing romances for fifteen years because she loves happy endings as much as her readers do. A former French teacher, Judy now devotes herself to writing full-time. She hopes readers have as much fun reading her stories as she does writing them. She spends her spare time reading, watching her favorite sports teams and keeping track of her two daughters. Judy's a native Texan, but now lives in Arizona.

CHAPTER ONE

BILLS. Bills. And more bills.

Abby Stafford sighed as she flipped through the mail. In the kitchen, dinner waited to be cooked, and in the living room Robbie watched TV impatiently. She could hear his favorite show blaring as he sang along in a high-pitched, slightly off-key voice.

If it weren't for the snack she'd given him, he'd be trailing her around the apartment like a puppy dog looking for his dinner. Robbie was only four and a half, but she affectionately referred to him as "the bottomless pit." Just like his daddy, she thought. Still, he was the center of her world.

A knock on the door interrupted her as she flipped through the phone bill. It had to be Gail again. No matter how many times Abby had told her neighbor she wasn't interested in a double blind date, the woman didn't seem to get it.

She swung open the door, not bothering to lift her eyes from the printout. "I've told you before, Gail, I'm not going."

"And I'm not Gail."

The timbre of the voice was unmistakable, the slight drawl too familiar. Before she could even look up, the mail slipped from her hands, floating softly to the wood floor. Abby thought she was going to follow it, albeit with a much harder landing.

The past had caught up with her. The man she'd loved since she was sixteen had finally turned up on her doorstep.

"Wh-what are you doing here?" She hadn't seen Nick Logan in five years, since his father's funeral. Since the death of Robert Logan had destroyed their marriage plans. Destroyed their dreams of moving to Cheyenne and leaving behind Sydney Creek, the small farming town where they'd both been raised.

She let her eyes light on him. They feasted on Nick like a hungry cowboy at a campfire. From his dark hair to his booted feet, the man had only gotten better with age. His tall frame was filled out with muscles now, thanks no doubt to the ranch work, and his brown eyes had crinkles at the corners, probably from working out in the sun all day.

Nick, too, took his time assessing her as held his Stetson in his callused hand. "I'm visiting you," he told her. But his voice wasn't pleasant. It was harsh, hard like him. He was exhibiting none of the gentleness with which he'd treated her years ago.

"I—I didn't know you were in town." It was all she could get out.

"Yeah. When Julie wrote me a letter about all the help you'd given her, I thought I should come say thanks."

It had been her pleasure to help Nick's sister; they'd been friends years ago. "That's very kind of you, but—"

"Don't get me wrong, Abby. I don't feel kind." He took a small step toward her. "I'm damn mad!"

"Wh-why?"

"As if you don't know."

She knew, but she wasn't going to admit anything unless she had to. So she lied. "No, I don't. And if you're going to be so rude, you can just go away for another five years!" She stepped back and grasped the edge of the door, ready to slam it in his face, when Robbie's voice startled her.

"Mommy, is dinner ready yet?" he asked as he came into the hallway.

Abby saw Nick's hard, dark eyes transfer from her to the boy. Instantly they softened. "Hi, there. I don't think I've met you. What's your name?" Nick asked, squatting down on his haunches as she'd seen him do a hundred times around a campfire.

"My name's Robbie. Who are you?"

Abby felt the world shrink to the three-by-six hallway. Her body tensed and she had to strain to get the words past the lump in her throat. "Nick, don't. Please."

His gaze flickered over her, and though she saw no emotion or empathy there, he replied, "I'm a friend of your mommy's. My name's Nick." He stepped forward and stuck his big hand out to the little boy. "Glad to meet you."

Robbie shook his hand. "Are you a cowboy?" he asked, his eyes big.

Abby didn't think her son knew much about

cowboys. She'd avoided the subject, but just the other day his preschool teacher had read them a story about a dog that helped a cowboy round up a herd. Robbie hadn't talked about anything else since.

"Yeah," Nick replied, "I'm a cowboy. Do you like cowboys?"

He nodded. "Do you ride a horse?"

"Sure do. Want to come ride with me?"

Robbie looked up at his mother. "Can I, Mommy?"

Despite the eager look on her son's face, Abby quickly said, "No! You have to go to school tomorrow, honey." She tempered her tone and urged him to go wash up for dinner.

Nick obviously didn't take rejection well. He called the boy back. "Before you go, Robbie, I wanted to ask you something. You look mighty big. How old are you?"

That was the one question Abby didn't want the boy to answer.

"I'll be five in— How many months, Mommy?"

Abby didn't respond. Instead she ushered him down the hall. When she turned back, alone, she prayed Nick was gone, gone back to the oblivion he'd lived in for almost five years. But the man was still there, his broad shoulders filling the corridor.

"Why didn't you tell me?"

There was no use denying it. Besides, she owed him an answer. "You told me to go have a life in the big city, remember?" She tried but failed to keep the bitterness out of her voice.

"I didn't know you were pregnant!"

"I didn't, either," she yelled back.

Nick drew a deep breath and ran his hand through his thick, dark hair. "You could've called me, Abby. This is the twenty-first century. There's all kinds of ways to contact a person."

She stood up to him, pulling herself up to her full five-seven frame. "Why? So you could be overwhelmed even more? You already had your mom hanging on to your shirttail and five other Logan kids depending on you. Did you need another?"

"Dammit, Abby, he's my son! Could I ever turn him away?"

"No, just his mother." She averted her gaze, unable to look at him. Things had been so bad back then after Nick's father had died. Responsibility and duty sat firmly on his shoulders, weighing him down, leaving him nothing to offer Abby, the woman he'd supposedly loved.

"Abby, I was trying to do what I thought was best for you."

She turned back to him. "Oh, really? And who put you in charge of me?"

He looked perturbed. No one challenged Nick Logan. His word was usually followed to the letter of the law. But Abby didn't back down. She held her ground and stared him down.

"You wanted to stay in Sydney Creek and clean house and cook for the whole brood, after you'd just graduated college?"

"I wanted to be given a choice."

Nick shook his head. "I couldn't let you do that,

Abby. You'd worked too hard to get your degree and you had a job waiting for you in Cheyenne."

"So did you."

"But I had responsibilities. Don't you understand that I had to do what I did?"

She nodded. "Just like I did."

"By keeping my son from me for almost five years?" The anger in his voice was barely in check, in deference to the boy just down the hall. But his eyes beaded and the lines at the corners became more pronounced.

Abby didn't want this to turn into a screaming match. She stepped back from him and drew a deep breath. "I think you should leave, Nick."

"Like hell I will!" he ground out in a hushed voice. "You've had Robbie for the last five years, now I get him for the next five." He looked around him. "The city is no place to raise a child."

Abby felt as if he'd reached inside and ripped out her heart. Breathing became difficult and the room started to spin. "No! No, you can't take him! He's my child. He doesn't even know you."

"And whose fault is that?" Nick's tone was menacing now.

Abby wouldn't cede him that point. She continued to shake her head. "I've taken care of him every day of his life. You can't just walk in here and wrench him away from me! You've got to give me time to—"

Nick gave her nothing. He leaned toward her, his face mere inches away. "I'm going back to Sydney Creek in the morning and I'm taking my son with me. Whether you come with us is up to you."

With that, he turned on his boot heels and stomped out her apartment as abruptly as he'd entered, leaving devastation in his wake.

Sitting in a fast food place, Nick hefted a half-pound juicy burger up to his mouth and weighed his options.

He could get a motel room and get a good night's sleep before the ride home tomorrow. But how could he be sure Abby wouldn't pack the essentials and slip away with his son in the middle of the night?

If it were him and someone was going to take his child away, he'd run. Still, he was too angry at Abby to consider her feelings.

No, on second thought, he really had no choices. He knew what he had to do.

He wrapped up his burger, grabbed his coffee and headed for his truck. He didn't stop till he was parked in front of Abby's apartment building. This was where he'd spend the night—right in front of the only exit. He wasn't giving Abby any chances to escape with his only child.

He'd never expected to be a part-time dad. Growing up, he'd remembered there'd been kids in school who had to deal with that situation and it tore them up inside. He wouldn't accept that for his son.

He'd expected to share his life with Abby, and their children. Back in Sydney Creek, they'd grown up as neighbors and the best of friends—until he'd kissed her on a dare when she was sixteen.

After that, they were a couple. Inseparable.

He'd followed her around faithfully and they'd even gone to the same college. He'd loved her more each day.

Holding off on making love to Abby was the most difficult thing he'd had to do then, but he'd promised his father he'd be responsible.

And he was—until the night they'd graduated, their diplomas in hand and a great life in front of them.

Two days later his father had died. With him, Nick and Abby's dreams.

His mother needed help with the Logan ranch and Nick's five younger siblings. Nick had no choice but to stay. But Abby did. As much as she'd imagined a life beyond Sydney Creek, Nick had to let her go. He remembered the day she left as if it was yesterday, not five years ago. It had tied for the worst day of his life.

Despite her attempt to make him feel guilty, he still felt it had been the right thing to do.

Except he hadn't known she was pregnant.

Through the window of the truck he stared up at the window of Abby's apartment. He could only imagine now the fears she must be facing. Was she sleeping? Holding Robbie in her arms? Crying her eyes out?

He had to stop feeling sorry for her. She should've told him he was a father. She should've come back to the ranch and lived with him. They could've raised their child together. That thought stopped him cold. The last five years would've been so much better if he'd shared them with Abby.

In his mind's eye he saw her when she'd opened the door to him earlier, looking as beautiful as he'd remembered. Her light brown hair had grown longer, falling in waves down to her shoulders. Still slender, she had the curves of a woman now. The urge to touch her, to feel her

against him, assailed him, taking all his willpower to withstand. He'd had to tuck his hands into the back pockets of
his jeans so she wouldn't notice the shaking. But he had
to resist her. He'd come for his son. Truth be told, he
wanted Abby, too…but she'd kept his son from him.

It suddenly struck him that she called the boy
Robbie. His father's name had been Robert Logan. His
eyes teared up at the thought. Years ago they'd talked
about their future children and toyed with names. He
hadn't really thought of naming a boy after his father
until after his sudden death. He'd never had a chance to
voice that to Abby.

But she'd done it for him.

Okay, so he owed her.

But that didn't mean she could keep his kid from
him.

Nothing could keep his son away.

"Mommy, I'm sleepy!" Robbie complained early the
next morning as Abby tried to juggle two suitcases, her
car keys, a bag and her son's tiny hand.

"I know, sweetie, but we're going, um, to visit a—a
friend of Mommy's." She hated lying to him. "When we
get there, I'll let you watch TV as much as you want
today." And she could wish her life had gone differently.

She and Nick had had such great plans. Living and
working in Cheyenne, marrying. She'd have had
someone to lean on, to share troubles with. They
could've raised Robbie together, taken him to Sydney
Creek to visit, taught him to ride, about life on the ranch.
Instead it had only been her, raising Robbie as a city kid.

The boy looked up at her, sleep in his eyes and a frown on his face. "But, Mommy, you said I always have to go to school. 'Cept on Sundays and Saturday. Is it Saturday?"

"No," she replied distractedly. This was no time for Robbie to chatter. It was already six o'clock and she had to get out before Nick came back. She shuddered to think what would happen if he found them leaving.

But she couldn't lose her son.

She'd slept maybe an hour last night, too busy to sleep, too scared not to. After packing up their things and arranging her finances, she'd wanted some sleep for the long drive she'd anticipated this morning. There was no "friend" to visit. She planned to put Robbie in the car then put as much distance as possible between them and Nick.

But Robbie proved harder to wake than she'd anticipated. He still lagged behind.

"Did we eat breakfast, Mommy? 'Cause I'm hungry."

She nearly dragged him, finally walking out the front door of the building now. "I know a great place for breakfast, sweetie. You'll like it. You can have pancakes."

"Can I have some, too?" a gravelly voice asked from behind her.

She didn't need to turn around. Her heart stopped and her shoulders slumped. She'd finally gotten her son outside and now their escape was thwarted.

After a moment she looked over her shoulder and there he was, leaning against the brick wall beside the front door. He struck a casual pose but she knew he felt nothing but irate.

"Hello, Nick. I—I can explain."

"I bet you can. But let me." He looked down at the

boy. "Hey, Robbie, did your mom tell you that you're going to my ranch? There's lots of cows and horses."

Robbie's brown eyes, so like his father's, danced between the two adults. "Really? Mommy, that's great! Are there dogs there, too?"

"You bet there are. Come on, buddy, I'll show you."

"Mommy, we'll have so much fun. Do you like horses, too, Mommy?"

Before Abby could speak, Nick interjected, "Your mommy isn't coming."

Robbie stopped dancing around, the excitement draining out of him. "Why?" he asked with a frown.

Nick squatted down to his level. "Well, she has a job, you know. It's real important to her, so she doesn't want to miss it."

Robbie looked up at her. "Mommy?"

Abby could no longer stand there and watch this drama. She broke through the paralysis that fear had brought on and went immediately to her knees in front of her son, her world. She looked into his watery eyes. "Nick's wrong, honey. Nothing is more important than you. Remember what I always told you? Where you go, I go."

"Yeah, Mommy. I remember. I'm glad 'cause I want to see the horses and dogs, but not without you." He slung his arm around Abby's neck, smiling now.

Abby tried to hide the tears that swamped her eyes, but failed.

"So you're coming with us?" Nick asked. "What about your job?"

She looked up at him and shrugged. "I'll wait and see how things work out." He might get tired of having guests after a few days. Or his mother might. Besides, she wouldn't admit that her job wasn't what she'd hoped for. Having graduated with a business degree, she'd hired on as office manager in a prestigious law firm, but left after two years over a personality conflict between her and one of the partners. Her new job, for a smaller company, wasn't challenging enough, but she'd decided to stick it out because it gave her time to spend with Robbie.

Nick gave her an odd look that made her feel uncomfortable, as if he were assessing her response. Then he shrugged and hefted her suitcases. "Come on, then. Us men are hungry, right, Robbie?" he asked, grinning at the boy.

"Yeah. Us men, Mommy!"

Abby hesitated, then grabbed the bag she'd dropped, along with her car keys. "I'll take my car and follow you. And I think Robbie should ride with me. His car seat is in my back seat."

Nick leaned closer to her and said in a low voice Robbie couldn't hear, "You're not planning on running away from me, are you?"

She stiffened and gave him an indignant glare. "I wouldn't endanger my child with a high-speed chase."

"Fine, then. I'll just hold your suitcases hostage until we get there."

Her suitcases? He'd already held her heart hostage for five long years.

"I know, Mr. Johnson, and I apologize, but the emergency wasn't planned. I have to go back home today."

Nick worked on his pancakes, listening to Abby as she spoke on her cell phone a couple feet away.

"No, sir, I can't postpone it. I have—" There was a pause before she said, "Yes, sir. I see." She flipped the phone shut without saying goodbye.

Nick looked at her when she returned to the table. "Mr. Johnson didn't take kindly to your emergency?"

She picked up her coffee mug. "He fired me. Are you happy?"

"Doesn't matter to me. Coming was your choice."

She pressed her lips together before she took another sip, then turned to her son. "Finished, Robbie? Let's go clean up in the rest room."

Nick stood up and offered his hand to the boy. "I'll take him to the men's room. He's too big to go to the ladies' room with you."

"Is it okay, Mommy?"

From her expression he expected her to protest. Instead she surprised him. "Yes, honey, it's okay." She knew Nick would never hurt him.

Robbie took Nick's hand. "What's it like in your room, Nick?"

"My room?"

"You know, the boys' room. I never been in one before."

Nick smiled. "Well, let's let you go see for yourself."

They walked toward the back of the restaurant, Nick holding his hand. "This is almost like having a daddy, isn't it?" Robbie asked, catching Nick by surprise.

"Uh, yeah, I guess so."

"I asked Mommy for a daddy, but she said she couldn't order one out of a catalog," the little boy said with a giggle.

"Didn't your mommy ever talk to you about your daddy?"

"No, I don't have one. Mommy always says, 'It's just you and me, Robbie.'" He giggled again.

And again Nick felt the anger build inside him. Abby could've told the boy something about— Well, maybe not. At least she hadn't said that Nick hadn't wanted his son.

When they emerged from the rest room, Abby was anxiously watching for her child. She immediately checked his face. "Did you wash the syrup off?"

"Yeah. Nick helped me. Mommy, it's different from your bathroom. They have uri-uri—"

As he stumbled over the word, Abby steered him out. "We'll talk about that in the car, sweetie."

Nick couldn't help but grin as he watched the boy walk away. He wanted to tell Robbie that he was his daddy, but he didn't want to upset the kid.

His kid.

For the first time he thought about what was going to happen when they reached the Logan ranch. His mother didn't handle surprises well. And Patricia?

Damn, things weren't going to be as easy as he'd hoped.

Robbie fell asleep after only a few minutes on the road.

Good. Abby needed to think. She'd spent so much time guarding her speech and screwing up her courage to face Nick that she was tired. Now she had to deal with what she would be facing in a few hours.

Not *what*, necessarily. *Who*.

Mrs. Logan.

All during the time that Abby dated Nick, she'd never felt welcome in his family home. His mother, in particular, had made it clear that Abby wasn't good enough for her son.

Abby understood that. She'd been raised on a small farm in the ranching community of Sydney Creek. Though her parents had worked hard, they'd never had much. During high school Abby had worked at the town café so she could buy her own clothes. On the contrary, the Logans, owners of one of the largest ranches in the area, lived a life of privilege and comfort. Nick and his family had things Abby didn't, like the new truck Nick had gotten when he'd turned sixteen.

Abby hadn't owned a car until she left for Cheyenne. It had been secondhand. And she still drove it. That wasn't likely to change anytime soon, she figured, now that she'd lost her job.

Actually Abby had been longing to go back to Sydney Creek, where she called home. But the thought of having to face Nick always kept her in Cheyenne.

Now that she was returning, her first priority was finding a job. Not an easy task in Sydney Creek, where only a few businesses thrived. For Abby, though, employment was essential; not only did she have Robbie, but she also helped support her mother, who had moved to Florida.

When her dad had died only a year after Abby finished college, her mother had moved to Cheyenne to live with her and Robbie. Susan Stafford had taken care of Robbie for his first two years, but when a friend of hers was moving to the Florida sunshine, Abby had to let her go.

Robbie went into day care, a clean, pleasant center only a few blocks from her job. He'd thrived there, made friends, some of whom went up to preschool with him.

Would she be able to find a pre-K in Sydney Creek? For that matter, would Nick allow Robbie to live with her in town? Or did he expect the boy to live with him at the ranch? Would he want her there, too?

Amidst the barrage of questions that assailed her, one stood out.

Did he still have feelings for her?

Abby had been shocked by how much she'd responded just to the sight of him. Seeing him at her doorstep yesterday brought back each and every memory of their time together—especially their graduation night. After years of denial and restraint, they were finally able to make love, to share the passion they'd held in check.

It had been five years ago, but seeing Nick made it feel like yesterday. She'd wanted to touch him so badly. But his attention had been all on Robbie. Not that she could blame him. After all, Robbie was the center of her world, too. She knew she was prejudiced, but he truly was such a good boy. He behaved himself, and he tried to take care of her whenever she got down and cried. That hadn't happened often, but when it did, he would come pat her shoulder and ask her what was wrong.

Never in this world would she let her son down. Nor would she abandon him, no matter what Nick promised.

She'd find a way to make it work. She had to, for Robbie's sake.

* * *

When they reached the ranch, Abby sat in the car, drawing a deep breath. The rambling single-story ranch house with its wraparound porch looked the same, as did the mountains in the background. She felt the same trepidation as she did the last time she'd seen it.

But she couldn't sit in the car for the rest of her life, so she let out the breath she was holding and woke her son.

"Robbie? We're here, sweetie. Wake up."

The little boy struggled awake. "Where are we, Mommy?"

"We're at Nick's ranch."

Instantly alert, Robbie strained in his car seat to look out the window. "Can you see horses and dogs?"

"Well, I hear some dogs—" She stopped when Nick suddenly jerked her door open.

He loomed over her, his hands on the roof of her small car. "Aren't you going to get out?" Without awaiting her reply, he leaned in and asked Robbie, "Ready, champ?"

"Yeah!" He clicked open his car seat and exited the car.

As Nick started to move away, Abby reached out and touched his hand.

"Nick, what are we going to—to say to your mother?" She didn't have to explain; Nick knew what she meant.

"We won't have to say anything," Nick whispered fiercely. "She remembers what I looked like at this age. That's why I didn't have to question you about his age. I knew I was his daddy as soon as I saw him."

"But your mom might say something—"

"Don't you think it's about time someone did?"

Abby's heart seemed to stop. "I don't want Robbie upset!"

Nick left her standing by the car door. "It's too late to worry about that." Then he walked off with Robbie's hand in his.

She scrambled to follow him. Regardless of what Nick said, she didn't want Robbie to learn the truth without her there to help him understand.

Despite Robbie's wails about seeing the cows, Nick insisted they go into the house first.

Abby knew Julie was in Cheyenne, and she'd guess Brad was out of college by now. If he'd come back home, there'd be at least four of Nick's siblings here to contend with.

She followed Nick and Robbie into the shadowy coolness of the house straight to the large kitchen where the family spent most of its time. Kate Logan was standing at the cabinet preparing something. "Who is it?" she called over her shoulder, obviously having heard them come in.

"It's me, Mom," Nick said.

She spun around, eager to greet her oldest son. But she came to a complete halt when she saw Abby with him. Her smile disappeared. "I didn't know you were bringing Abby to visit, Nick."

"I brought Abby and her son to visit."

Kate noticed the little boy for the first time. Her eyes widened in shock and she immediately looked at Nick. "Is he—"

Abby held her breath, waiting for her to blurt out the secret she'd kept all these years.

But all Nick said was, "This is Robbie, Abby's little boy."

After looking at Abby for a moment without speaking, Kate knelt down to Robbie. "Hello, Robbie. I'm pleased to meet you. I'm glad you've come for a—a visit."

"Thank you," Robbie replied, displaying all the manners Abby had ever taught him. "Nick says he has horses and dogs."

"Yes, he does. In fact, one of the dogs had puppies a couple of weeks ago. Would you like to see them?"

"Real puppies? Not play puppies?"

"Real puppies. I'll get Nick's brother to take you." She stood and said, "Nick, call Brad."

Nick went to find his brother.

"Mommy, do you want to see the puppies, too?" Robbie asked. She should have known he'd be a bit nervous about a stranger taking him.

She smiled to let him know it was okay. "You go with Nick's brother. I'll come out later, sweetheart. I'm tired. I didn't get a nap in the car like you."

He leaned against her leg, his hand taking hers. In a whisper, he said, "But I don't know Brad."

Abby knelt and hugged her son. "I know, but I do. He's a lot like Nick. He'll never hurt you, either."

The young man in question walked into the kitchen, a smile lighting up his handsome face.

"Hi, Abby. It's good to see you."

"You, too, Brad. This is my son, Robbie."

"Hey, Robbie. I hear you want to see the puppies. I

might even be persuaded to let you hold one. How about that?"

"Really?" Robbie asked with enthusiasm, immediately taking Brad's hand.

"You two go ahead and I'll have lunch ready when you get back," Kate said.

After they left the house, Abby said, "So much for him not wanting to go without me."

"Only because you told him Brad was someone you knew. I appreciate that, Abby," Kate said, surprising Abby.

She only nodded, waiting for what would come next. She knew it wouldn't take Kate long to get to the point.

True to form, she asked, "So, you had Nick's child?"

"Yes."

"Now what, Nick?" Kate asked her son.

"I told her she'd had Robbie for the first five years of his life so now I get him for the next five."

Kate looked aghast at her son's words. "No wonder Abby came with you!" She shook her head. "What about Patricia? Have you given thought to how she'll react to this news?"

Abby looked from one to the other. "Who is Patricia?"

Nick took an indignant stance. "She doesn't have anything to do with you!"

"Son," was Kate's only word. But it seemed to have an affect on Nick. He turned away and began pacing the room.

The realization dawned on Abby and she felt as if her heart lurched. She looked at Kate. "Don't tell me she's his wife."

CHAPTER TWO

"SHE's not my wife!" Nick exclaimed, spinning around.

"Then who is she?" Abby asked.

"She's my fiancée."

Not that big a difference, Abby thought. Holding her emotions in check, she asked, "Have you told her about Robbie?"

"No, not yet. But she won't mind," he snapped.

Abby had her doubts about this Patricia. And it gave her an opportunity to negotiate with Nick.

"Look, Nick, I agree you need to get to know Robbie. But I've come back to Sydney Creek. I intend to stay here…as soon as I find a job. Let me find a place in town to live and you can spend the weekends with Robbie."

"No!" Nick ground out. "He stays here! I—"

He broke off his tirade when they heard the arrival of Brad and Robbie. The little boy ran into the kitchen to his mother, babbling about the puppies he'd held and which one was his favorite.

"I liked the littlest one best, Mommy. He was so cute."

"You want to have that puppy as your own?" Nick asked.

Robbie's eyes got big. "Can I? Mommy, can we take the puppy home with us?"

"Tell him!" Nick ordered.

Abby sank down to her son's level. "Um, sweetie, we're going to be staying here for a little while. As long as we're here—"

"Tell him the truth!"

"What's he want you to tell me, Mommy?"

Abby closed her eyes. She'd dreamed of this moment so many times, played it out in her mind. But telling Robbie who his father was never went smoothly. She'd always anticipated having more time to get the script right. Apparently she was wrong.

Help came from an unlikely source. It was Kate who protested. "You're being too hard on her, Nick."

Nick didn't answer his mother. He merely stood over Abby, never taking his eyes off her, waiting.

Abby knelt down before her son. "Honey, do you remember asking about your daddy?"

"Yes, but it's okay, Mommy. Don't cry again."

Abby tried to hold back the tears she could feel in the back of her eyes. How much she loved this boy! "No, I won't cry. But—but I— Your daddy—"

Suddenly Nick knelt down beside her. "I'm your daddy, son. I didn't know about you or I would've come for you sooner."

Robbie's brown eyes took on a confused look. "Are you sure? 'Cause Mommy said I didn't have a daddy."

Abby took his hands in hers and spoke up, though her throat was tight and her eyes welled with tears. "He's right, Robbie. Do you know where I got your name?"

He shook his head.

"Your grandfather died just before I went away. When I found out I was expecting you, I wanted you to have something to remember about him, so I named you after him. His name was Robert, too." Tears were streaming down Abby's face now, but she didn't care.

"He never saw me when I was a baby?" Robbie asked.

Abby felt a hand on her shoulders. Kate had come forward to stand beside her. "No, darling, he didn't," Kate said, clearly emotional, "but he would if he were here. He was my husband, and Nick's daddy."

Robbie turned to look at Nick. "You had a daddy?"

"Yeah, I did. He was a real good dad. And you have a grandma."

"I do?" Robbie asked, not making the connection.

"I'm your grandma, sweetheart," Kate said.

"Wow. There's lots of us, Mommy. This is going to be fun!"

He never ceased to amaze Abby. She'd fretted so about telling him, but Robbie wasn't upset. He marveled at the idea of having a huge family.

But "fun"? She hardly thought being in Sydney Creek with Nick and the other Logans would qualify as fun. But she couldn't tell her son that. She looked down at the floor, trying to figure out what to say.

"Isn't it good, Mommy?"

Of course it was, she told herself. For Robbie. She looked up and forced a smile. "Yes, of course, sweetie."

"So we're going to stay here and I can have my puppy?"

"You'll have to ask your grandma. It's her house," Abby said, hugging her son.

"But, Mommy, you're going to stay, too, aren't you? You're my mommy!"

Before Abby could think of an answer, Kate spoke up. "Absolutely, your mommy will stay. She's part of the family!"

Nick raised his voice in protest. "Mom, what are you—"

Hands on her hips, Kate held her ground. "It is my house, isn't it, Nick? I say she stays."

Nick stared at her a moment, then he spun on his heels and walked out of the kitchen.

Abby was speechless. And confused. *Kate* had come to her defense? As for Nick, he clearly wanted nothing to do with her. Regardless of his mother's insistence, how could Abby stay? "Kate, maybe it's best if—"

"No. This is all my fault. I won't allow him to separate you from your child!"

"What do you mean it's all your fault?"

Before Kate could respond, Brad put his hands up. "I don't think I want to hear this." He started for the hallway. "I'll go find Nick."

Abby didn't know what to say. Stunned, she could only stand there, watching Kate wipe the tears from her eyes.

After a moment, Kate began to explain. "I thought Nick could do better. You probably realized that. Then when his father died, I didn't want him to go away. I— I needed him. So he missed out on Robbie's life. And…and now there's Patricia!" Kate said, bursting into more sobs.

Abby looked down at her son. "Robbie, go watch something on television for a few minutes."

"Okay, Mommy, but is Nick really my daddy?"

"Yes, sweetheart, he really is."

"Okay. I'll go think of a name for my puppy!"

"Now, Kate," Abby said, leading Nick's mom to a seat at the kitchen table. "My getting pregnant wasn't your fault. And no matter whose fault it was, I would never give Robbie back. I love him so much."

"Of course you do, Abby. And he's absolutely perfect. But—but I could've managed without Nick. I *should've* managed without Nick. Then the two of you would've been together."

"You'd just lost your husband and you had five other children depending on you. You couldn't have done it all on your own. Look, Nick and I have already had this argument. He made the decision for both of us. I let him do that, but he didn't have that right. And I didn't believe in his love. So we all share the blame. But it's water under the bridge."

"Oh, Abby, you're being very generous."

Abby ducked her head. "No, not really. I'll admit I blamed you a little, too. But in the end, it was Nick who sent me away. It took me a while to stop being angry."

Kate stiffened. "I realize he shouldn't have—"

"No, we need to just let it go. Our time is gone. Now it's Nick and Patricia's time. I can accept that as long as he doesn't take Robbie away from me."

"I won't let him do that, Abby, I promise."

"I want you to tell me if my staying here causes problems between you and Nick. I'll start looking for a place at once."

"No. I know Nick is upset, but he can't be that mean.

I won't let him force you to leave your little boy here while you go away. Robbie would hate him if he did that."

"Maybe not if he gets that puppy!" Abby said with a small smile through her tears.

"Yeah. He's just like his daddy, isn't he?"

"Yes. I'm sorry I kept him from you, Kate, but I didn't— I didn't know how to come back."

"Well, that's certainly one thing Nick accomplished," Kate said with a shaky laugh. "A grandson! And you named him after Robert. That was so wonderful of you."

"I'm glad you're pleased."

"Oh, yes." Kate patted a chair next to her for Abby to sit. "Now we've got to find a place for you to settle in. Let's see. Julie is in Cheyenne, so you can have her room. We'll put Robbie in Charlie's room. He's at college in Laramie. It's right next to Nick's room, so that should please him."

"Perfect, Kate. Thank you for making me feel welcome."

"You're the mother of my grandson. Of course you're welcome."

Much as she was still surprised by Kate's transformation, there was still the big question looming over them. "Now we have to talk about Patricia."

"Oh."

Abby stared at Kate. "Is she that bad?"

"Well, she's very pretty…in a prim way."

"What do you mean?"

"She expects everything to go her way."

Abby stared at Kate. "With Nick? She gets her way with Nick?"

"No. She's playing him very carefully. But everything else is done her way or not done at all. She volunteered to cook for Nick once. He agreed, thinking she'd come out and fix dinner for all of us. But she fixed dinner just for her and Nick. And she didn't even fix enough for him. He works hard all day. You know how hungry he gets. He was polite to her, but after she left, he fixed himself a sandwich!"

"And where did you and the kids go to eat?"

"To the café. Julie and Brad weren't here. The other three didn't care. They thought it was great. When we got home, I found she hadn't had time to wash the dishes. She left them for me!"

"She didn't!" Abby protested.

"Yes, she did. When I got home, Nick was trying to clean up and eat his sandwich at the same time. I took over. But that's when I realized I'd made a big mistake. She's totally wrong for him!"

"Does she like children?" That would be the woman's saving grace, that she would be good to Robbie.

Kate slowly shook her head. "I know she's a teacher, but she doesn't seem to— The kids don't like her."

"Maybe she's better one-on-one?"

Kate slowly shook her head. "No, I'm afraid not."

Abby sank back into her seat. She'd vaulted one hurdle—Nick's mother—but the more formidable one loomed ahead.

What was she going to do about Patricia?

The topic of Patricia didn't come up again for the rest of the day. Abby was too busy to worry about her. After dinner, she helped Kate clean the kitchen. Then she gave Robbie his bath before dressing him in his pajamas.

Though she hesitated, she encouraged him to go tell everyone good-night. Kate hugged him and gave him a kiss. Then Robbie looked at his mother. She nodded in Nick's direction and Robbie walked over to Nick to tell him good-night.

"Don't I get a hug like your grandma did?" Nick asked.

"Okay," Robbie said.

After Nick hugged him, Robbie moved on to Brad and his two younger brothers who had been introduced to Robbie when they'd returned home from school. Then he turned toward Abby, his hand outstretched for her.

"I'll carry you to bed, Robbie," Nick said, scooping him up before he could protest.

"Okay," Robbie said, but his gaze centered on his mother. "Mommy, are you coming?"

"Yes, sweetie, I'm coming."

Nick glared at her, but she ignored him. Her son wanted her to come, and that was all that mattered.

She followed them into Charlie's room, the one that now would be Robbie's room.

Nick put Robbie down on the bed.

Abby reached for the covers and pulled them back. "Here you go, sweetie. You're going to like this room. It's right next door to your daddy's."

"Where is your room, Mommy?" Robbie asked.

"I'm right down the hall. Don't worry, I'll be here when you wake up in the morning."

The boy settled into the bed. "Will you go see my puppy in the morning?"

"Yes, I will. Did you decide on a name?"

Robbie looked at the man looming over his bed before he looked back at his mother. "I—I want to call him Baby. 'Cause he's the littlest one."

Abby looked at Nick. To her relief, he said, "That's a good name, Robbie."

The boy smiled, as Abby leaned down to tuck the covers around him just the way he liked.

"Now it's time to say your prayers," she told him.

He folded his hands together for their nightly ritual. As Abby said the prayer, he repeated the words. Then he added his own requests at the end. "Thank you for my puppy, and please bless Mommy and—and Daddy."

With a smile, Abby bent over and kissed him goodnight again.

Nick didn't move. He stood by the bed, an odd, contemplative look on his face. He was about to say something when the phone rang. He looked toward the kitchen where the closest phone was located.

"Nick, Patricia is on the line," his mother called.

Without saying anything, Nick turned and left the room.

"Is he mad at me?" Robbie whispered to his mom.

"No, he's not. He just had to go take that telephone call. Everything's fine. Don't you worry."

He nodded. "Mommy, are we really going to live here?"

"I'm not sure. But we'll be together, you and me, just like always."

"Okay," he said and closed his eyes. "G'night, Mommy."

She smoothed his silky hair. "Good night, baby."

But instead of leaving him, Abby sat beside his bed, not eager to go back to the kitchen. Kate had been more than welcoming, but Nick seemed to be angry all the time.

His brothers were friendly enough, especially toward Robbie. Brad had introduced him to Matt, who at thirteen was thrilled to no longer be the baby. Then to Jason, who at sixteen had his mind on more important things than a new nephew.

Abby smiled, remembering Nick at sixteen. That was when he'd first kissed her.

Life had certainly changed a lot in the next seven years. By then she was alone in the city, without Nick. And she was pregnant.

She looked down at the boy now breathing more deeply as he'd drifted off to sleep, and kissed him lightly on the forehead. She wouldn't change anything.

She tiptoed out of Robbie's room.

The crowd in the kitchen had thinned down to only Kate and Nick. He was still on the phone and Kate was baking a cake.

Abby stepped to Kate's side and whispered, "Is there anything I can do to help?"

"No. You've already made my day easier."

"I'm glad." Abby smiled at her, till Nick's loud, angry shout startled her.

He yelled "No!" into the phone and slammed it down.

Abby stared at him, but she knew better than to say anything. She didn't look away but she remained silent.

Kate did the talking. "Is something wrong, son?"

Reining in his temper, Nick looked first at her and then Abby. "No, nothing's wrong." And he stalked out of the kitchen.

When she was sure he was out of earshot, Abby asked, "What do you think just happened?"

"I think Patricia just discovered the true Nick. She's been nudging him along, but he wouldn't budge tonight."

Because of her? Abby wondered. And Robbie?

"Kate, don't you think it would be better if Robbie and I lived somewhere else?"

"No. I want to get to know my grandchild, not just have him visit every once in a while. If it brings Nick to his senses, all the better. If it doesn't, I suspect she'll force him to build them another house."

Abby shrugged "If he does that, I guess he really loves her."

"I'm not so sure," Kate said, staring into space.

Abby's heart beat faster. She hadn't admitted to herself how much she wished Nick would want her again. She hadn't admitted how much she still cared for him. The reality was that he was engaged to another woman.

A woman who would be her son's stepmother.

Nick slammed the door to his bedroom behind him. He guessed he shouldn't have expected Patricia to take his news well. Any fiancée would have trouble learning about a son she hadn't known existed.

But now that Robbie was in the picture, things had changed.

And what about Abby? She was free...and the mother of his child.

He cautioned himself from going down that road. He was supposed to be angry with her for keeping such a precious secret from him. But maybe he understood her reasons.

He'd always understood Abby.

It was different with Patricia. They weren't soul mates. He knew she liked his money and status in the community. And there was no great passion between them, not like with Abby. He hadn't made a push for her to commit emotionally. Physically, either. He'd tried to tell himself that would change once they were married.

Now he had to find a way to deal with Patricia and his son. And Abby. Clearly she wasn't going anywhere. He knew she'd never abandon her child. As long as he kept hold of Robbie, which he intended to do, no matter what, he'd have Abby living here.

He'd have to make sure no one else came sniffing around her.

He frowned. Where had that thought come from?

Still, he couldn't help wondering if she'd had boyfriends in Cheyenne. She was as pretty as ever, and as sweet. It would seem unlikely that she hadn't had men wanting to be with her. Unless Robbie had kept them away. For the first time, he saw Robbie as more than just his son. He'd also been a watchdog for his mother.

Lying back on his bed, his hands behind his head, he contemplated the future. After a while, he gave up and shut off his light.

Who knew what the future would bring?

* * *

Robbie got up at seven the next morning, his regular time, despite the fact that it was Saturday. As she'd promised, Abby was waiting for him in the kitchen. She'd gotten up earlier to help Kate make breakfast.

Nick had ignored both of them, but Brad had commented on how well they worked together.

When Robbie entered the kitchen, Kate hugged him and asked if he was hungry.

He looked at the display of food on the table. "Pancakes! My favorite!"

Abby looked at her son. "I laid out some clothes for you, Robbie. Why didn't you get dressed?"

"But I don't have to go to school now," Robbie explained.

Abby, however, didn't cut him any slack. "Go get dressed. Then you can have breakfast."

Robbie looked at Nick, as if he thought he would overrule Abby. Nick simply said, "Do you need some help?"

"No, I can do it, 'cept tying my shoes."

"I'll do that for you when you're dressed," Nick promised him.

After Robbie left the room, Abby whispered, "Thank you."

"For what?" Nick asked.

"For not overruling me. He knows to get dressed, but I guess he wanted to test me."

"I'm in favor of rules. I won't interfere unless I think you're telling him the wrong thing."

She nodded and continued working on the breakfast.

Five minutes later, Robbie returned to the kitchen, dressed in the clothes Abby had chosen for him.

"My, don't you look nice," Kate praised him.

"Thank you...Grandma." He eyed her as if wondering if she would accept her new role.

"You're welcome, grandson."

He looked at his mother. "Is that me?"

She smiled. "Yes, it is, sweetie."

Robbie went to Nick. "Daddy, will you tie my shoes now?"

"Sure. Come here." Nick lifted Robbie to his lap and tied his shoes. "Now, how about a man's breakfast?"

"Mommy, can I have a man's breakfast?"

"How about a little man's breakfast?" Abby offered. With a grin, Robbie nodded.

They all sat around the table a little longer than usual. With Robbie there, Nick seemed to relax more and even smile now and then. She enjoyed the time and even began to feel welcome.

Until the back door opened and a tall, thin, tawny-eyed blonde came in.

Abby didn't need Nick's exclamation to know this was the infamous Patricia.

"Patricia! I didn't expect you," Nick said, rising to greet her.

In spite of the audience, or perhaps because of it, she said, "Hi, lover," and put a liplock on him that Abby found embarrassing. A look at the others showed the same reaction.

Nick took her arms from around his neck and broke off the passionate kiss. "Patricia, the family is here."

"Hi," she said, with a smile that didn't include any of them.

Kate stood up, scraping her chair. "Sit down, Patricia, and I'll pour you a cup of coffee."

She tossed her long mane of silky hair. "Here? Oh, no, Nick and I like to be private."

"Pour her some coffee, Mom. She'll join us." Nick's voice was firm and he pulled out a chair for his fiancée.

"Nick," Patricia said, pleading in her voice, "we need to talk."

"Later. Let me introduce you to my son. Robbie, this is my fiancée, Patricia Atwell."

Without even an acknowledgment, she asked Nick, "What's his last name?"

Nick turned to Abby.

"His name is Stafford," Abby replied.

"You didn't list me as the father?" Nick demanded.

"Yes, I did, but it seemed easier for him to have my name."

"In that case I'll start adoption proceedings at once," Nick returned, no doubt in his voice.

"But, Nick, we haven't even talked about this," Patricia whined. "You already have to pay child support. Are you sure you want to adopt him?"

"He's my child, Patricia. I'm responsible for him." Nick sent a smile to Robbie, ignoring his fiancée.

"I still think we should talk about this, Nick," Patricia said, her voice gentle, but to Abby her eyes looked hard.

"No," was Nick's only response.

Once again Kate tried to defuse the volatile situation.

"Uh, Patricia, have you had breakfast? I'm sorry, I should've asked when you first came in. I can—"

"Oh, no, thank you, Mrs. Logan. I had my usual breakfast earlier."

"Do you want to see my puppy?" Robbie suddenly asked. "Mommy is going to come see it. Uncle Brad said I could bring it into the house in a week."

Patricia looked aghast, her manicured hand going to her chest. "In the house? Oh, I would never allow animals in my house. They make too much of a mess."

"But Grandma said—"

"It's okay, buddy," Nick said softly. "You can bring your puppy to the house when it's big enough."

Patricia was clearly not satisfied. "Nick, you don't want to set a precedent. You should explain to him now that I won't—"

"This is my mother's house, Patricia, and that won't change."

"Oh. I see," she said and smiled, as if she'd won a contest.

Next to her at the table, Brad jumped up from his chair. "Uh, I have to get to the barn and see about a sick horse."

Abby could understand his desire to run. She shared it. "May Robbie and I walk with you, Brad? I promised him I'd go see the puppies."

Jason and Matt decided to go with them, too. Soon the kitchen was empty of everyone but Nick, Patricia and Kate.

"Why don't we go to your office while your mother does the dishes, Nick?" Patricia suggested.

Nick squared his jaw, a sure sign to Kate that her son was digging in his heels. "I've got a better idea. Why don't we help Mom clean the kitchen?"

CHAPTER THREE

ABBY was stunned by the performance she'd just seen. She walked beside Brad toward the barn, unable to speak, unable to focus on Robbie's chatter as he strode ahead with Matt and Jason. The scene in the kitchen replayed twenty times in her mind.

"Excited about Nick's future wife?" Brad finally asked.

Abby looked up in surprise. "Do I hear sarcasm in your voice?"

"Come on, Abby. You must see how poorly matched she is to Nick. If he marries her, his life is going to be a living hell!"

The thought had crossed her mind, too, but she wouldn't voice it. Instead she said, "Obviously something attracted him to her. You have to give them a chance, Brad."

"Not me. If she moves in, I move out."

"I would guess she won't move in. I can't see her living with the family." In fact, Abby felt sure that wouldn't happen.

"So you think he'll dump her?" Brad asked, a happy note in his voice.

"No, that's not what I meant. I think Nick will build her a new house."

"Damn! I hadn't thought of that."

"Brad, Nick has to make his own choices. That's the only way he'll be happy."

He shook his head. "Either way, I doubt he'll be happy with Witch Atwell."

Abby grinned, just as Robbie called from inside the barn. "Aren't you coming, Mommy?"

Realizing she and Brad had come to a stop, she sent him an apologetic look and rushed into the barn to see the puppies.

"See, Mommy?" Robbie said, holding up a tiny black and white puppy. "This is Baby."

"Oh, he looks sweet, Robbie. It is a he, isn't it?" she suddenly asked.

Jason took the puppy from Robbie and did a quick anatomical check. "Uh, no, it's a girl."

"Does that mean I can't call him Baby?"

"No, Robbie. That means you can call *her* Baby," Abby said with a smile.

Robbie carefully took the puppy back from Jason. "Mommy, did you know Jason and Matt are my uncles, but they're boys, too?"

"Yes, dear, I realized that."

"I didn't have even one uncle yesterday and now I have three!" Robbie couldn't contain a big smile.

"Four, actually. Charlie is away at school. And you have one aunt. You've always had them, Robbie," Abby pointed out. "I just hadn't told you about them."

"Oh. And now I have a puppy, too!"

Abby looked at the three Logans in the barn with them. "Don't ask him which he is most excited about. I'm afraid you'd lose to the puppy."

"We know, Abby. We love puppies, too," Matt told her with a grin. Then he frowned. "But Patricia isn't going to let us have puppies in the house."

Abby kept her mouth closed. It wasn't her place to try to reassure Nick's young brothers.

Brad didn't seem to feel the same way. "Abby thinks she'll insist that Nick build her a new house."

Matt frowned. "So that means Nick can't live with us anymore?"

"Yeah," Brad muttered. "It means Nick is being led around by his—"

"Brad!" Her gaze flew to her young son, but he was too engrossed in his puppy to see her panicked expression. "What it means, Brad, is that Nick wants to please his future bride. That's an admirable trait in a man."

"Yeah, that's what I meant," Brad told his brothers, but he rolled his eyes at Abby.

"Shall we go back to the house now, Robbie? I think your puppy needs more time with his mommy. Put him back and you can come out to see him again tomorrow."

"Where's the sick horse?" Robbie asked.

Abby turned to look at Brad.

"Uh, there isn't one. That's kind of code. We use those words to say we've got to go. Patricia doesn't know that, so she's not offended when I leave."

Robbie started to ask another question, but Abby decided her son had asked enough questions for one morning. "Come along, Robbie. We need to go help Grandma clean up the kitchen."

"Okay."

When they reached the house, they discovered Kate doing the dishes by herself. Abby immediately apologized.

"Don't worry, Abby. It's the way it's been since Julie left home. Just me and a lot of men who are no good at dishwashing."

"Maybe you should be training them," Abby said. "It would make them better husbands."

Kate laughed. "I could just imagine how they'd react to that idea."

"Well, while I'm here, you've got a willing helper."

"Thank you, dear."

"Where's my daddy?" Robbie asked.

"Oh, he's in his office with—" Before Kate could finish her sentence, Robbie was running down the hall.

"Is Patricia still here?" Abby suddenly asked.

"Yes."

"Oh, dear, I'll be right back." She hurried after Robbie but hadn't gotten out of the kitchen when it was already too late.

"Get out of here, you little monster! How dare you walk in on Nick and me!"

Abby didn't stop until Robbie flew into her arms, tears streaming down his face.

"Mommy, she yelled at me!"

Abby picked Robbie up and brought him back to the kitchen.

"Sweetie, you forgot to knock. Anytime a door is

closed, you need to knock and wait for whoever is in the room to tell you to come in. You can't just open the door and walk in."

"I forgot!" the boy said through his tears. "I thought Daddy would want to know!"

Nick entered the kitchen and Abby was surprised by his concerned expression. He knelt and reached out for Robbie.

"What would I want to know, son?"

"I wanted to t-tell you Baby is a girl. I'm sorry I forgot to knock."

"It's no big deal, Robbie. Ladies just get upset about little things."

"Mommy doesn't," Robbie said, frowning at his father in confusion.

"That child needs to be taught some manners!" Patricia announced from the doorway. "Obviously his mother hasn't done a good job."

Abby was going to tell her what she could do with her rating of Abby as a mother, but fortunately Nick intervened.

"Abby has been a wonderful mother and will continue to be. What you fail to understand, Patricia, is that Robbie is only four years old."

"Oh, really, Nick, it's obvious he's been spoiled. It wouldn't take many days with me to instill some discipline in him. Believe me, my classes are well-behaved."

"You teach high school, Patricia. Give him another ten years and he'll be better behaved, too." Nick hugged Robbie before he stood. "You okay, son?"

"Yes, Daddy," Robbie said, but he buried his face in Abby's lap.

From the doorway, Patricia groaned. "Nick, must he call you that? It's going to cause all kinds of rumors. It would be better if he called you Nick."

Kate stepped forward, intending to answer that question, but Nick put a hand out to stop his mother. "No, Patricia, that won't do. Robbie is my son and I'm not embarrassed about it. I didn't bring him home to hide him."

"I can't figure out why you brought him here at all. Then to move his mother into the house is just absurd! People are going to say you're having an affair. That's an insult to me! Though, of course, they would find it hard to believe that you'd prefer someone who has let herself go as much as she has."

"Dammit, Patricia, would you think before you say things like that? You've managed to insult me, Robbie and Abby already this morning. Anyone else you want to complain about?"

She opened her mouth and Abby held her breath.

"Don't even think about it, Patricia!" Nick obviously read her response before she spoke.

She tightened her lips in a disdainful manner and started for the door. "Well, if you don't want my wisdom, then I might as well leave. I'll see you this evening." She slammed the door behind her.

The kitchen remained silent, as if its occupants wanted to be sure she was gone.

"Mommy, who is she?" Robbie whispered.

"She's going to marry your daddy," Abby whispered back. She realized how much she had been trying *not* to believe that would happen, but if Nick was tolerant of her behavior today, Abby knew she had to give up whatever hope she had had. Unadmitted hope, it was true, but she couldn't hide from herself anymore.

"Nick, surely you're not going to marry her," Kate finally said.

"Why not, Mom? You wanted me to date her. You thought because she's a home ec teacher that she'd know how to cook and keep house."

"Hell, bro, that's not what's important in a marriage!" shouted Brad, who had followed his older brother into the kitchen. "She's going to drive you crazy!"

Nick shrugged his shoulders.

Abby had to speak up; it was the perfect moment. "Nick, you need to let me and Robbie find our own place. I didn't fight you about coming back because I wanted to come back. But living here with you will cause talk, like Patricia said. I won't object to your having Robbie out to the ranch when you want, but—"

"No!"

His thunderous response shocked everyone, freezing them in place.

"Son, you're not thinking. If Abby wants to move to her own place, how can you stop her?"

"I can't," he said in a booming voice. "But I can go to court and get custody of Robbie!"

"No!" Abby shrieked. "No! I won't give Robbie up!"

Nick strode toward her, stopping mere inches from her. His eyes were small and dark as he speared her with his gaze. "Then don't talk about moving away. Besides, when you get a job, you'll need Mom to take care of Robbie."

Abby stared at the man in front of her, unable to comprehend him. "You—you can't ask that of Kate!"

"The hell I can't! She's my mother. And I didn't bring Robbie back for him to spend his days in day care."

"No, you brought him back so your mother could run a day care in her spare time!"

Kate stepped in between them. "Children! It's okay, Abby. I'll enjoy spending time with Robbie. He'll spend most of his day in school, and I'll have Matt and Jason to help me in the afternoons, if you're still working."

"I—I have to, Kate. Mom depends on me to send her money each month. I can't—"

"Of course not. Don't worry about it."

Abby was deeply concerned about what Nick had done to his mother's life. She understood why he had dragged her back home. She had made the decision not to tell him about his son and she needed to pay back that debt. But now Kate would have to pay, too.

Like an angry bull, Nick headed for the door. Before he went through it, however, he paused. Without turning around, he said, "We'll enroll Robbie in school on Monday." Then he disappeared.

"'We'? What does he mean by that, Kate?"

Kate put her arm around Abby's shoulder. "He means he's going with you, just in case you don't tell them he's the father."

Abby's throat felt parched, her cheeks flushed. "Patricia will be furious about that."

Kate smiled. "Yes, she will, won't she?"

"Why do you look pleased about that? I don't want to upset her!"

"But you won't be. You didn't ask for Nick to go, did you? And you certainly have no control over him. After all, you're not his fiancée, are you? So don't worry about it."

"But—"

Kate's hand tightened on Abby's shoulder. "Child, now you know why I greeted you with open arms. The main reason is that I misjudged you long ago, and for that I'm sorry. But also it's because I can't stand Patricia. And I don't want Nick to be unhappy."

"Kate, I can't promise to do anything about Nick's situation. And I don't want him to sue for custody. I'm afraid I might lose, and I couldn't bear that!"

"It's all right, dear. I think I may go with you on Monday, too, just to keep the gossips somewhat quiet."

So there were four of them in Nick's truck Monday morning going to register Robbie for school. The boy sat in the second seat, clutching his mother's hand, Nick noticed through the rearview mirror.

Earlier, at breakfast, Robbie had asked him if he could go back to his old school in Cheyenne.

Nick, while patient, had explained that it was too far to drive.

Robbie had immediately assured him his mother wouldn't mind.

Nick smiled at the memory as he pulled up in front of the school that catered from preschool through elementary.

"Come on, Robbie. We're here," he announced as he got out of the truck and held open the back door of the dual cab.

Robbie hesitated, tugging Abby after him. Suddenly, Nick leaned forward and took hold of Robbie, surprising him so that he turned loose of his mother's hand.

"Wait! Mommy, are you coming?"

"I'm right behind you, Robbie. Grandma's coming, too."

Robbie kept his gaze on the two women. Nick thought the boy liked him well enough, but more often than not, he needed the comfort of his mother's presence.

Inside the small school, Nick led the way to the Principal's Office. When he stepped inside, a familiar female voice greeted him.

"Why, Nicholas Logan, what are you doing here?" Mrs. Andrews, one of Nick's teachers when he'd attended the same school, and now the principal, looked down at Robbie. "Well, now, who is this?" she asked gently, reaching out to take Robbie's hand.

"Can't you tell by looking?" Nick asked.

"I'd guess yours if I didn't know better." She paused to look behind Nick. "Hello, Kate. And…Abby? Is that you? Well, what is this? Old home week?"

"I've moved back to Sydney Creek, Mrs. Andrews, and I want to enroll my little boy in prekindergarten."

Mrs. Andrews flashed her eyes at Nick before she responded to Abby. "That's great, Abby. I thought I'd never see you again after your father died and your mother moved away."

Nick stepped forward to interject. "What Abby failed to mention is that Robbie is *my* son, too, Mrs. Andrews."

"Yes, I could tell. Well, Robbie, come in and let's talk."

She reached for the boy and saw his eyes dart to his mother. "She's coming, too, but she's too big to sit at my special table."

That caught Robbie's attention and he loosened his hand from his father's hold.

Nick watched as Mrs. Andrews led Robbie to a little table with kid-size chairs. Robbie immediately reached out to touch the intricate Tinkertoy structure in the middle.

"I like this."

"I can tell. Did you have toys like these at your school?"

"Yes."

"Look at these. I have lots of colors here. Do you know which colors are which?"

Robbie nodded at once. "That's red. I like red."

"Me, too," Mrs. Andrews said, putting Robbie at ease. "And this one?"

"That's blue. It's Mommy's favorite."

"Yes, I remember. And this one?"

"That's yellow. My teacher said it was the color of the sun, but the sun is really orange."

"I think you're right. And this one?"

"Green. That's what trees and grass are—unless it doesn't rain. Did you know that trees drink the rain?"

"Yes, I did. Who told you?"

"Mommy. She tells me lots of things."

"I see. And does she read to you?"

"Every night. And sometimes extra times 'cause our television doesn't have anything good on it."

"I knew I did a good job teaching your mommy!" Mrs. Andrews said with a laugh. "Did your mommy teach you to be polite and mind your teacher?"

"Yes," Robbie said before he dropped his head and muttered. "Once I had to stand in the corner, but I said I was sorry."

"Good for you. I think you'll like our class here. Would you like to go meet some of the children your age?"

"Yes! Do they have puppies, 'cause I have a puppy!"

"Do you really?"

Robbie didn't even look back as he and Mrs. Andrews left her office.

Nick was frowning. "Is that it? Don't we have to fill out forms and things like that?"

"I'm sure we will when Mrs. Andrews returns, Nick, but we don't need Robbie for that."

"Well, is he going to stay all day? I was going to show him the horses today."

Kate leaned forward. "He'll get out of school at two, Nick. He can probably work it into his afternoon."

The principal walked back into her office, a smile on her lips.

When she was behind her desk, she pulled some forms out of a file and handed them to Abby. "Fill these out, dear. You've done a fine job raising him."

"Thank you, Mrs. Andrews."

"What about me?" Nick demanded.

"I assume you just found out about him, or he

would've been here sooner. But he'll do well. He's settling in just fine in the classroom."

"How many students do you have in Pre-K?" Abby asked as she filled out the forms.

"Robbie will be the sixth one in the class."

"That's all?" Abby asked. "I had no idea he'd be in such a small class."

"Maybe we should keep him home this year and bring him next year," Nick suggested, suddenly unsure.

"No!" Both Kate and Abby protested.

Mrs. Andrews turned to him. "Nick, excuse me, but I understood you were engaged to Patricia Atwell. Was that just gossip?"

"No," Nick growled, staring at his hands.

"Then, I think the decision remains with Abby."

"Dammit! I'm his father and he's living with me!"

"I thought he was living with Abby," Mrs. Andrews said, staring at the threesome in front of her desk. "Just what exactly is going on here, Nick?"

CHAPTER FOUR

ABBY felt her face growing hot. "Uh, Mrs. Andrews, I'm living with Kate right now, until I can find a job and—"

"You're not taking Robbie away!" Nick roared.

Mrs. Andrews looked between the two parents. Then she turned to Kate. "Can I ask you to take your son to the café and buy him a cup of coffee? We'll be through here shortly and Abby can join you."

In spite of Nick's protests, Kate agreed at once and pulled her son after her. Once the door was closed behind them, Abby braced herself for whatever Mrs. Andrews wanted to say.

"Abby, are you aware that you have control of your son? That Nick cannot just decide that he wants his son to live with him?"

"Yes, Mrs. Andrews. I never told Nick about Robbie, and he's very angry about that. He's threatened to sue for custody. I—I don't want to take the chance that he could take Robbie completely away from me."

"I don't think he'd win," Mrs. Andrews said, "but I can understand your reasoning. Are you aware of his engagement?"

Abby ducked her head. "Yes, and I've met the lovely Patricia."

Mrs. Andrews chuckled. "I'm sensing a little sarcasm, my dear, and I don't blame you. But that only makes her a more difficult foe."

Abby faced her former teacher. "I'm not fighting her. If Nick chooses Patricia, then that's his problem, not mine. If, as I suspect, she forces Nick to build her a separate house, then I think Kate might not mind if we continue to live with her. I'll be glad to pay rent after I get a job."

"I see. I guess Kate would love for you to rout Patricia."

"That's not what I'm trying to do. I just want to be with my son and keep him safe and happy."

Mrs. Andrews nodded. "I see. All right, then, just finish filling out those forms and we're done. Your son will get out of school at two o'clock. Oh, do you have money for his lunch today? You'll find a form in there to pay for a lunch card, so he won't have to handle money."

"Good." She handed over the two dollars for that day's lunch and wrote a check for a lunch card to start the next day. Then she finished filling out the forms.

After handing them over, she extended her hand to Mrs. Andrews. "I just want to thank you for being so understanding and making Robbie's first day a good one."

"It's my job," she said with a smile. "Let me know if there's any way I can help in the future."

Mrs. Andrews was a dear, but Abby doubted the principal could give her the kind of help she need.

When Abby reached the café, she saw Kate sitting in a booth by herself. Nick was nowhere in sight.

"Did you lose your son on the way over?"

"After he got me situated, he walked over to the general store to order more feed. He'd forgotten he needed to do that. Is everything okay?"

"Yes. Mrs. Andrews was afraid Nick was running roughshod over me. I explained his threat to sue for custody and that I didn't want to take a chance on losing Robbie."

"Does she think Nick is terrible?"

"Of course not. She's known him for years. I explained that he was angry. But, Kate, it occurred to me that if Nick builds a house for Patricia, would you mind if I continued to live with you? I'd pay rent. At least I would as soon as I find a job."

"I'd love to have you stay, Abby, and rent wouldn't be—"

"Did I hear someone is looking for a job?" a crusty voice said behind Abby.

She whirled around to find the owner of the café, George Kirby, her old boss, standing behind her. "George!" she exclaimed and slid out of the booth to hug the elderly white-haired man. "How are you?"

"I'm better for seeing you, little Abby."

"I'm no longer little, George. I grew up while I was in college." She thought George had shrunk a little more since she'd seen him.

"You needin' a job?"

"Yes, I'm afraid so. I've come back here to live with my son, and I have to send money to my mother."

"Well, I could use some help."

"I need to find a job that covers the hours my little boy is in school."

"What's the hours?" he asked.

"Eight in the morning until two in the afternoon."

"I could do with someone from six a.m. to two p.m. Could you manage that?"

Kate offered, "We can get Robbie off on the bus with Matt in the mornings, Abby. You lay out his clothes each morning. It wouldn't be a problem. And I haven't heard of any other jobs available around here."

"You could take the job on a temporary basis until you see if it works out," George suggested, giving her options. "After all, you've done it before."

Abby smiled at them both. "All right, George, I'll take it."

"Great! Can you start in the morning?"

"That soon?"

"I've been having to do both the cooking and the serving lately. It cuts down on how much business I can handle."

"Well, then, I can start in the morning. Thank you, George, for making it so easy."

"You're a good waitress, Abby. I know what I'm getting."

He brought out another cup and filled it with coffee for her.

"Well, that problem is solved," Kate said with a smile. "I hope I didn't force you to take the job, but there really haven't been any others available. That's why Julie went to Cheyenne."

"I meant to ask you if she's found anywhere to live?"

"No, I talked to her day before yesterday and she was still staying with those friends."

"Would she be interested in subletting my apartment?"

"How much?" Kate asked, sitting up straighter.

"Eight hundred a month, which would mean four hundred each if she found a roommate. Anything they don't want to use they can just put in a box. I'll drive back to town in a week or two and pick up what they don't want."

"We'll call as soon as we get home. I've got her work number. I know it would be a big relief. And I think she's found someone she wants to room with."

"Good."

"What's good?" Nick asked, scooting into the vinyl booth next to his mother.

"Abby is willing to sublet her apartment to Julie and a friend," Kate explained. "Isn't that wonderful?"

"Yeah. Just great."

But Abby thought he sounded less than pleased.

"If you don't want me to offer my apartment for some reason, just say so, Nick."

"I don't care what you do. When's George going to bring me some coffee?"

"I'll get it," Abby said, sliding out of the booth. She went behind the counter and got a clean cup. "George? I'm serving Nick some coffee."

"Sure thing!" he hollered back through the opening to the kitchen.

"You shouldn't have done that," Nick said when she'd poured him coffee. "George pays someone to do that job."

"Yes, me."

Nick glared at her. "What are you talking about?"

"George offered me a job. I accepted."

"That's ridiculous! You didn't go to college to go back to waitressing!"

"It's all that's available. I'm not going back to Cheyenne without my son, Nick."

"You could probably get work in Pinedale," Nick said with a scowl.

"And spend an hour driving each way? No, thank you."

"Abby, you're not thinking," Nick returned. "You can do better than this!"

"I'm not ashamed of my past, Nick. And working here with George will allow me to pick up Robbie from preschool and have the afternoon at home with him."

"That's my job!"

Kate elbowed her son in his ribs. "With all the work on the ranch, you'd make that schedule for a week at the most. Then you'd be sending me in to pick him up. I think Abby's smart to take this job and have more time for Robbie. She's his mother."

"Maybe he could go to Patricia's room and stay there until I picked him up," Nick said. "The schools are right next to each other."

Together, Kate and Abby said, "No!"

"Why not?"

"Patricia obviously doesn't like little children, and it's not—"

"Of course she likes kids. She's a schoolteacher!" Nick shot back.

Kate laughed and then wiped her smile away as her son glared at her.

"It doesn't matter, Nick. She's still not responsible for my child. I am."

"I'm responsible, too!"

"Yes, you are, but you aren't available in the middle of the day. I am."

"I don't like it!"

"I didn't ask for you to like it. It's just the way it is." Abby picked up her coffee and took a sip.

Then she looked at Kate. "Is this the way the coffee usually tastes?"

"I'm afraid so. A lot of people still come here, because it's about all we've got, but George has slipped up on a few things."

"Well, I'll take charge of the coffeemaking in the morning."

"You'll have to get here really early to do that," Nick pointed out, as if that would discourage Abby.

"I'll be here at six o'clock. That's when I'll make the coffee. It will be ready by six-thirty, when we open."

"What are people going to say when they see you waiting tables?" Nick demanded.

Kate looked at Nick. "I think Patricia is rubbing off on you. What does it matter? It's honest work and gives Abby time with her son."

"You're both prejudiced against Patricia."

"I have nothing against her as long as she's kind to Robbie," Abby said quietly.

"Of course she'll be kind to Robbie," Nick insisted.

"As long as he remembers to knock?" Kate pointed out.

"We wanted to be private, Mom. That's not normal for us."

Abby said nothing. Then she looked at her watch. "I need to make preparations for tomorrow. Can we go now?"

Nick immediately said, "I was thinking about getting a piece of pie." He leaned back in his seat and stared at Abby.

"Certainly, Nick. What kind would you like?" Abby said, not bothering to point out that he only wanted the pie to go against what she wanted.

Nick looked over at the glass case that held the pies George bought from a local lady who baked them fresh every day.

"I think I'll have the apple. What about you, Mom?"

"I might as well have some pie, too. I'll have pecan."

After Abby had gone to get their desserts, Kate said softly, "I think Abby will do very well here. At least she'll make good coffee and serve people with a smile."

"She'll regret taking the job. It's not an easy one."

"So you think being a single mother is a job for people who like things easy?"

"No, Mom. I know you've had to be strong."

"But you're wrong, Nick. I had it easy. I had enough income and I had you to lean on. Abby didn't have anyone."

"She could've told me. I would've helped."

"After you sent her away? I don't think she believed in your love after that. And it's a good thing she didn't since you're now engaged."

"Hey, I didn't make any promises."

"Yes, you did. You promised to marry her."

"Abby knew I had no choice at that point. And she didn't argue. She did what she wanted to do."

"I think she did the only thing you left for her to do."

Abby arrived back at the booth with the pie. "Here you go."

They all three heard the cowbell over the door ring, signifying another customer, actually two.

Instead of sitting down, Abby walked over and greeted the two men. "Good morning. Can I get you something to drink?"

"What's she doing?" Nick demanded in a whisper.

"She's helping George out. What did you think she was doing?"

"George should've come out and helped them."

Kate took a bite of pie and chewed slowly.

"Hurry and eat your pie, Mom. We need to get Abby out of here."

"But she's doing just fine."

"That guy's flirting with her."

"So, she'll get a better tip."

Nick got up from his seat. "Come on, Abby. We need to go."

"In just a minute," Abby said. Then she turned back to the two gentlemen and wrote down their orders. "I'll give this to George and he'll get your food out to you in just a few minutes."

After she gave George the orders, she walked back to their booth and cleared the table, carrying the dirty dishes to the kitchen.

"Nick, are you paying?" she asked as she reappeared.

"Yeah, why?"

"I'll ring it up for you," she said calmly.

"Fine," Nick said, sounding like he was grinding his teeth.

He slapped a ten-dollar bill down on the counter. "Keep the change!"

She gave him a cold, level look and slipped the bill into the cash register. Then she turned to smile at the two diners. "Enjoy your meal, gentlemen," she said as she stalked out of the café, the cowbell echoing her angry departure.

Nick said nothing until they were in his truck. Then he glared at Abby in the rearview and demanded, "Why didn't you keep the tip?"

She kept her gaze averted. "I wasn't working today. I was just helping George out."

"I intended the tip for you."

She looked up, her icy glare nearly frosting the rearview mirror. "I don't need your charity, Nick Logan. I've proven that I can take care of myself and my child without your help."

"Dammit, Abby!" Her reasoning managed to work its way past the wall of anger that he'd erected around himself. Though he didn't want to concede the point, he had no choice. "I'm still angry, but I know I owe you for taking such good care of Robbie."

Abby's eyes softened and he could practically see the tension seep from her upper body. She'd obviously been gearing up for a fight. After a moment she said, "It's all right, Nick. I'm living in your home and Robbie is getting to know his family. That's all that matters."

Nick cleared his throat. "Thanks, Abby. That's very generous of you."

He wondered if they'd just crossed a major hurdle in their new relationship.

Robbie had crossed the biggest hurdle.

He'd gotten past his first day at school. That evening, during dinner, he talked incessantly about how much fun he'd had.

Abby was thrilled. She knew the first day was always the hardest, whether it was at a new job, in a new family, or a new school. Eventually, though, she had to interrupt her son's endless chatter. "Robbie, I'm glad you had a good time at school today, but maybe you should give someone else a chance to talk, too."

Robbie looked around the table. When no one spoke up, he opened his mouth to continue, but Abby forestalled him. "How was your day, Matt?" she asked.

Like a typical teenager Matt kept his reply to a minimum. "Okay." He shoved a forkful of mashed potatoes in his mouth. "But I did get a hundred on my math test."

"Why, that's wonderful," Abby exclaimed.

"Yes, I'm very proud of you, son," Kate said. "I'd been wondering, but I was afraid it was bad news since you hadn't said anything."

"I figured Robbie had a lot to say tonight."

"What did he say?" Robbie whispered to his mother.

"He said he made a really good grade on his test." She smiled at her son. "Isn't that good?"

"Yes, Matt, that's very good," Robbie said, sounding like his mother."

Matt's brothers all told him how proud they were of him. He looked embarrassed. "Jeez, I wouldn't have said anything if I knew you were going to make such a big deal about it."

"Yeah, you would've," Jason teased him. "We know you like to show off."

Matt protested and had to put up with a lot more teasing.

But Abby smiled genuinely at him. "Matt, I think you're setting a good example for Robbie, and I appreciate it. Besides, I'll know who to ask to help him when he reaches your grade."

"It's not like his dad could help him with anything, is it?" Nick put in, his sarcasm tempered by a helping of humor.

"Of course you could, Nick. I didn't mean you couldn't, but if you and Patricia live in another house, it might not be very convenient for you to—"

He put down his fork. "Wait just a minute, Abby. What makes you think I'm moving out of this house?"

"I thought— I guess I thought that because she seemed so pleased when you told her this was your mother's house, that you'd agreed to build her her own house."

"I didn't promise to build it. She wants me to, but I can't see doing that. This house is big enough for everyone."

"If I find a place in town to live, will you let me take Robbie with me when you marry Patricia?" Abby asked, still hopeful he'd come to his senses and realize how crazy it would be for the two of them to live under one roof.

"No. No one is telling me how I live."

"Aw, come on, Nick," Brad started, but Kate shushed him.

Then she said, "It's time to clean up. Abby has to bathe Robbie and get him in bed, and she doesn't have time to help with the dishes. So we're going to start something new tonight. You four boys are going to help, two a night, so I'm not stuck doing it all by myself."

There was a lot of protest, but not from Nick. "Mom's right. We need to help out around here." He looked at his brothers. "Matt and I will work tonight. Tomorrow is Brad and Jason's turn. Okay?"

"Yeah, sure, Nick," Brad agreed. He and Jason shoved back their chairs and hurried out of the kitchen.

"I could've helped, Kate," Abby said quietly.

"No, I've been thinking about what you said. I think I should've thought of this before now. And besides, after tonight, you'll be too tired."

"Then, thank you, Kate. And you, too, Nick and Matt," she said and led Robbie out of the kitchen.

Nick got up from the table, flinging a dishcloth at Matt. He shot him a big smile and said, "Okay, little brother, let's get to work."

His KP detail was the shortest on record. Just thirty seconds later, the phone rang.

CHAPTER FIVE

NICK answered the phone and Matt and Kate both knew he wouldn't be back to help. The caller was Patricia.

Matt did his brother's share and after Kate finished loading the dishwasher, she got the broom and began sweeping the kitchen. The sound of the phone being slammed down drew her gaze, but as Nick turned, she ducked her head and kept sweeping.

"Here, Mom, I can at least do that. I'll apologize to Matt later."

"It's okay. I told him you'd do all of it on your next night."

"Of course." He took the broom from her and picked up where she'd left off. "By the way, I'm sorry I didn't think of this sooner. All these years, you'd think I'd've figured it out."

Kate patted his arm and smiled at him. "You did fine, son. It's all right."

"Mom," Nick said as she started to leave, "can I ask you something?"

"Of course."

"What do you think of Patricia?" He watched his mother's expression change.

Then she said, "It doesn't matter what I think. It matters what you think, Nick. You're the one who will have to live with her, make children with her. I admit that I have wondered whether you love her, but I've decided it's none of my business."

"It will be if we live here with you and the others."

Kate sighed. "Yes, then it would be my business. I'm not sure Patricia is one who plays well with others."

"She's pushing for me to commit to building a new house for her."

"I see."

"I told her if I did that, Robbie would be coming to live with us."

"I don't think Abby will agree to that, Nick."

"She suggested Abby live with us, too. I was surprised by that, till she told me she'd already heard about Abby's job at the café. Patricia figured if Abby lived with us, she could be the maid."

Kate's eyebrows rose. "She expects Abby to agree to such a thing?"

"That's what she said. I think she's planning on Abby refusing and not letting Robbie come live with me. This way Patricia would come out smelling like a rose. In her opinion, anyway."

"Not in mine!" Kate exclaimed.

Nick shook his head and leaned on the broom. "Mom, I can't promise to build her a house."

Kate let out a sigh. "Then, I'll do my best to get along with her."

"I know you will, Mom."

"I can't guarantee to make her happy. I don't like people who sit on their hands while I do the work."

Nick looked sheepish. "Like your sons who haven't been very helpful?"

"Nonsense. You and your brothers work hard on this ranch. The housework's my area." She grinned. "Not that I mind a little help now and then."

Just as she finished speaking, Robbie flew into the kitchen to give a round of good-night kisses. "Daddy, I didn't know you were in here, too!" he said.

"I'm helping Grandma out," Nick said, showing his son the broom. "I was just taking a break."

Abby followed her son in. "I thought you might be in the TV room, Kate. Isn't this the night of your favorite show?"

"Oh, yes, I almost forgot! Give me a kiss, Robbie, so I can go watch television." She bent and hugged her grandson.

Robbie sagged against his father's chest. In a mournful tone, he said, "I wish I could go watch Grandma's favorite show."

"Nice try, kid," Abby said, "but you don't even know what it is. Come on. Tell your daddy good-night."

Nick went one step further. When Robbie stretched up to kiss him, he hoisted the boy in his arms. "I'll take you to bed tonight," he said.

Abby, who had turned to leave the room already, stopped in her tracks. Over her shoulder she said, "But aren't you sweeping the kitchen?"

Nick shrugged. "So I'll come back and finish it later."

Robbie looked so happy, she couldn't deny him the moment. No one had ever put Robbie to bed but her. Only she knew their nighttime ritual. Strange feelings she didn't want to identify coursed through her, and she turned away before Nick saw her face.

As he passed, he grabbed her arm. "You can join us, you know."

No further encouragement was needed. She followed the two males down the hall to Robbie's room.

Nick put Robbie on his bed, and Abby purposely kept herself back. She watched as he led their son through his nightly prayers and tucked him—not exactly the way she always did but apparently good enough for Robbie. He leaned down to kiss him goodnight and Abby couldn't help but well up with tears. Part of her was touched by Nick's affection for the son he never knew, while part of her was slightly jealous. Could he so easily replace her as the most important person in Robbie's life? Embarrassed by the thought, she ducked her head.

"Mommy, where's my good-night kiss?"

Robbie's sweet voice reached out to her, and she smiled up at him. She held her son in a tight hug and kissed his forehead, as she did every night. It was amazing how much she loved this child.

Before she left his bedside, she gave him instructions for the morning. "Matt will come wake you up in the morning. Make sure you get dressed before you go to breakfast. Then wash your face and hands and brush your teeth before you get on the bus with Matt. Okay?"

"Okay, Mommy."

She hugged him again. "And I'll be there to pick you up after school. Good-night."

She'd barely closed the bedroom door, Nick ahead of her down the hall, when he spun on his boot heel and started questioning her.

"Why is Matt supposed to look after Robbie in the morning?"

"Because he promised to watch out for Robbie on the bus. I just thought—"

He stopped her with an index finger to her lips. "In case you don't remember, Abby, Robbie is my son." He moved in closer, now only a foot from her.

All Abby could think about was how close Nick was to her, how she could feel the heat coming off his body. How in his dark brown eyes she could see the gold flecks that she'd always loved.

When he blinked, that magic spell was broken and she came to her senses.

Nick continued, "*I'll* make sure he's dressed for breakfast, and *I'll* make sure he washes up and brushes his teeth. *I'll* take him to the bus stop along with Matt and Jason."

When he lowered his finger, she replied, "Of course, if that's what you want."

His voice softened, probably because she wasn't fighting him on it. "Do you need me to wake you up, too, in the morning?"

"Uh, no, no thank you. I'll set my alarm." She gathered her composure and stepped back. "Speaking of which, I need to get up early so I'll say good-night now."

Nick didn't move back to allow her to pass. He stood his ground right next to her, looking down into her eyes, and Abby thought he was about to say something. In the end, though, he walked silently back down to the kitchen.

Abby went to her bedroom, shut the door behind her and leaned back on it. Drawing in one deep breath after another, she tried to still her nerves. Because ever since he offered, all she could think about was waking up to Nick's voice.

It reminded her of a time long gone.

A time that would never be repeated.

Abby sighed and changed into her nightgown. It was going to be a long night.

"You always were on time."

George checked his watch as he came down the stairs from his apartment over the café to let Abby in.

"I try, George," she said, covering a yawn with her hand. She'd managed only an hour's sleep last night, tossing and turning until the sheets looked like a pretzel.

George didn't appear much more alert. He hadn't shaved and his shirt was unbuttoned. "Why don't you go back upstairs and finish getting ready? I'll get things started."

After muttering his thanks, he went back up the stairs, and Abby turned to her first job. Making a pot of strong coffee to wake her up.

By the time George came down, she had blueberry muffins in the oven, pancake batter and scrambled eggs ready, and had begun to fry bacon and sausage. Onto the counter she put two plates of a hearty breakfast. "Order up," she called out to him with a smile.

Tapping two fingers to his forehead in a mock salute, George sat down to eat, Abby taking the seat next to him.

"Missy, you cook a good breakfast. And this coffee is lots better than I've been making."

"Thank you, George. I learned from the best," she said with a grin.

He shook his head. "I think maybe I've forgotten how."

George was up there in age, but Abby figured he was more likely overworked. "I can write up some recipes so you can refresh your memory. It will all come back to you."

"Yeah, I'd like that. Do you still make meat loaf from my recipe?"

"Of course I do. It's my son's favorite."

"Well, I need that one, too."

"I'll do them at night on a Rolodex so you can find them easily."

Just as they were finishing up their coffee, the first customers of the morning knocked on the door. George went to let them in and Abby took their dishes to the kitchen.

Four men came in sniffing the air. "What smells so good?" one asked.

"The coffee," George said succinctly. "Abby made it."

To a man, they all asked for a cup.

In no time the café was nearly packed. Abby and George worked like a well-practiced team, her pouring coffee and taking orders, him doing the cooking.

Business didn't slow till nine when she finally had time for a break.

"I can't believe you did this by yourself, George," she said, plopping into a chair.

"I didn't do it very well apparently. The café hasn't been this busy in over a year. Word must have spread right quick."

Abby refused the credit. "Well, now that it's slow, are you ready to put together some meat loaf? I can get a pan of it ready and put it in the refrigerator until lunch."

"Make two pans and I'll make it the featured item today," George said, rubbing his hands together.

Abby made the two meat loafs and put them in the refrigerator. Then she mixed up a pan of King Ranch Chicken Casserole, another recipe she'd learned from George, and some other easy dishes.

About eleven, the lunch crowd began. Again, it was much larger than George had been experiencing and Abby was grateful when Ellen, the other waitress, arrived. The coffee flew fast and furious, as did the meat loaf, chicken casserole and the other specials Abby made.

She was cleaning a table with her back turned when Nick came in with his brother Brad. They took a booth and Ellen appeared within a minute, ready to take their orders.

"No offense, Ellen," Nick drawled, "but I'd like Abby to serve us."

"She has the other half of the dining room, Nick. Don't worry, I'll take good care of you."

"Thanks anyway," he said, deflecting her flirtatious grin and getting out of the booth. "Come on, Brad, we'll go over there."

Brad followed his brother but after they sat down, he leaned forward. "What are you trying to do? Tell everyone Abby is your property?"

Nick gave his brother a stubborn look. "I want Abby to serve me. If you want to go back to the other table, feel free."

Just then Abby turned around to them, a pencil poised over her pad.

"Afternoon, gentle— Oh! Hi, Nick, Brad. I didn't realize you'd be in town today."

"Well, something came up. Some, uh, business to attend to," Nick supplied. "How are you doing?"

"Just fine. What can I get for you?"

"Did you make the coffee?" Nick asked.

"I did. Do you both want cups?"

"Yes, please. We'll be ready to order in a minute."

He never took his eyes off her as she got the coffee and brought them their cups. He picked up his cup and tasted it. "Yeah, definitely you made it."

"I don't lie, Nick," Abby said quietly, shooting him a look.

He wanted to call her on it. Maybe she didn't lie, per se, but she'd definitely committed a lie of omission. After all, she never did tell him about Robbie, did she? But this wasn't the time, nor the place. So instead, he ordered his lunch. Brad did the same.

"I'll be right back with your meals."

Again Nick kept his gaze on Abby as she went behind the counter.

"Stop staring at her!" Brad admonished him. "People are going to notice."

"I'm just trying to determine how tired she is. This is a tough job."

"She seems to be doing pretty good. She's lots faster than Ellen."

"Yeah, I guess." Nick looked around the café. "Seems most of the men are sitting in Abby's section, though." He was frowning.

"So? She'll probably get good tips."

"You sound like Mom."

"Nick, you should know Abby better than that. She's going to work hard at whatever job she has."

"Yeah."

Abby brought out their lunch. "Ellen is going to take care of you now. I'm going to work in the kitchen for a while. Let her know if you need anything."

"Why are you cooking? Where's George?"

"George is busy and so am I," she said and walked away.

Nick started up out of the booth and Brad reached across the table to grab his arm. "Where are you going, Nick? You can't chase her down in the kitchen. Let her do her job!"

Nick subsided into his seat. "Why can't she ever listen to reason?"

"What are you talking about?"

"I told her this would be too hard for her."

Brad stared at his brother. "Are you crazy? She seems to be doing a great job."

"She's having to do the cooking and the waiting on tables? That's ridiculous!"

"Again, she doesn't think so."

"How will she get through in time to pick up Robbie?"

"I suspect she'll manage."

"I don't think I should leave until she gets off work."

"Then you can get a ride home with her, because I need to get back to work."

"Fine. I'll catch a ride with Abby."

"Great. I'll go as soon as I finish my lunch and you can pay for it."

"No problem."

George wanted Abby to prepare two more pans of meat loaf, and anything else she wanted to make in her final hour at work. He'd serve everything that night.

Abby made the meat loaf and then a green enchiladas recipe she'd learned in Cheyenne and several other casseroles that she thought people would like.

"Okay, George, you've got four different casseroles and the meat loaf for dinner tonight. Okay?"

"Thank you, Abby girl."

"I'll write up some of the recipes this evening and bring them in tomorrow so any of us can make them."

"Bless you, child."

"Bye, George," Abby said, kissing his leathery cheek. When she came out from behind the counter, her apron off, she discovered Nick was paying his bill. "You're still here?"

"Yeah. Can I catch a ride to the ranch? Brad had to leave early."

Though she looked surprised, Abby agreed at once. "We have to go pick up Robbie, of course," she said.

"Of course."

"You're not checking up on me, are you?" she asked, looking at him out of the corner of her eye as they walked to her car.

"Of course not."

"Hmm. Okay." They got in her car and drove the short distance to the school. "Here we are. Robbie's supposed to wait until I come in to get him. I'll hurry."

Abby walked up the sidewalk, feeling Nick's gaze upon her as she moved. It wasn't the first time he'd watched her do something. But it still made her nervous.

"Mommy!" Robbie called out, running into his mother's arms.

"Hi, sweetheart. How was school today?"

"It was great! I took a test, too, and the teacher said I did good."

"Did well."

"What?"

"I'm sure your teacher said you did well."

"Oh, okay."

"Guess who's in the car waiting for you?"

"Grandma?"

"No, your daddy."

"Really? I thought Daddy had to work on the ranch."

"Usually he does." Though Abby had her doubts about his excuse today. "Come on, let's go."

When Robbie saw Nick, he dropped her hand and ran down the sidewalk to his daddy who was standing outside the car. When Robbie reached him, Nick swung the little boy up into his arms and gave him a hug.

Abby's heart lurched. To anyone observing them, they looked like a real family, a husband and wife picking up their child from school. To Abby, that was just a dream. A dream of what could have been—but never was. Never would be.

Thanks to Patricia.

As if her mere thoughts had conjured the woman, Patricia appeared outside the school. Her unmistakable, shrill voice called out to Nick.

"Did you make arrangements to meet her this afternoon?" Abby asked him.

He shook his head and put Robbie in the back seat. "Give me a minute." Then he strode forward to meet Patricia who flung her arms around him and, right there in front of everyone, kissed him on the mouth.

The kiss affected Abby more than she cared to admit. As much as she knew Nick belonged to Patricia now, seeing them as a couple was something else again. The image, she knew, would stay with her long after she closed her eyes for bed tonight.

"What's Daddy doing?" Robbie asked her.

"He's talking to his fiancée, honey. He'll be along in a minute."

"I don't like her," Robbie said.

"Don't say that to your daddy, honey. He loves her, so it would hurt his feelings if you told him that." Averting her son's attention, she said, "Tell me about your day at school."

"It was fun. And I have a friend. I sat with him in my class and on the bus because his big brother sat with Matt. His name is Johnny."

"That's wonderful, sweetie." She had worried how Robbie would make new friends.

"Here comes Daddy!" Robbie announced.

Nick got in the car and motioned for Abby to go. "Sorry I held you up."

"No problem, Nick."

"Patricia thought I was coming to see her."

"In the middle of the day? Aren't you always at the ranch?"

"Yeah."

Abby didn't want to talk about Patricia. Instead she steered the conversation to what she thought was safer territory. "Robbie made friends with a little boy named Johnny. He says his brother is friends with Matt. Do you know who he's talking about?"

"That's the Crawford family. I'd forgotten about them having a boy Robbie's age."

"Robbie, maybe Johnny can come home with you some afternoon and play," Abby suggested.

Robbie cheered that idea, but Nick, apparently, didn't share his enthusiasm. He shot Abby a scowl. "You're trying to do too much."

Abby ignored his protest.

"Did you hear me?"

"Yes, I did," she replied, flicking a glance his way. "But you're not in charge of what I do."

"I told you that job is hard. You need to give yourself time to adjust to it."

"Having done it part-time for four years, I think I know how difficult the job can be. But any job is difficult."

"At least you weren't on your feet so much in Cheyenne. And probably making more money."

"Money was always tight." She regretted it as soon as she said it. Nick looked immediately guilty.

"Do you need money? Do you have debts to pay off?"

"No, we managed okay. It just wasn't easy at times."

"Is there anything Robbie needs?"

"No, he's fine."

Nick turned to look at his son. "Hey, Robbie, do you have any cowboy boots?"

"No. Just my tennis shoes. Why?"

"I was thinking about buying you some real cowboy boots. We'll have to go to town on Saturday and see what we can find."

"Then can I be a cowboy like you?"

"Yes, son." Nick shot a grin over his shoulder. "And we probably need to buy your mommy some boots, too."

"No, thanks!"

"Anyone who lives on a ranch needs boots. For riding."

"I haven't done any riding yet."

"But you will this weekend. I plan to take you and Robbie for a ride. Come on, Abby. It'll be fun."

"We'll see," she said, hoping to put him off. After the visual reminder of Nick's engagement, spending more time with him probably wasn't a good idea.

Out of the rearview mirror, Abby could see Robbie grinning at his father, and Nick was looking at his son with the same expression. While she was glad Nick was pleased to have his son with him, being here made her life more difficult. But she'd endure the hardship, for Robbie. He should have the opportunity to know his daddy and his family.

As an only child, she certainly didn't have much to offer in the way of family. There was only her mother now, and she was two thousand miles away.

The key to making this situation work for Robbie was simple. She had to let the males bond while she kept her distance from Nick. The man she'd once loved more than life itself.

Once? Asked an inner voice.

She refused to reply, focusing instead on her driving until she arrived at the ranch.

When they entered the kitchen, Robbie went to play, pausing only to give Kate a hug.

Kate looked at her son. "Why aren't you out working? I thought you had those new cows to tend to."

"I decided to wait in town until Abby got off work and picked up Robbie."

"It gave him a chance to see Patricia, too," Abby added.

"During the middle of the day? That must've surprised her," Kate said.

Nick ignored the remark. "She's coming over tonight."

"For dinner?" Kate asked.

"I don't know. She wasn't too specific."

Abby had left the kitchen while he and Kate talked, giving them some privacy. Besides, she didn't want to hear any more about Patricia. When they were quiet, she came back in with a package.

"What did you buy?" Nick asked.

"A Rolodex for George. I'm going to write down the recipes I learned from him. His memory isn't as good as it once was. If he has it written down, he can still make things."

"That sounds like a lot of work, Abby," Kate said.

"It won't be too bad. I'll just do some basics tonight and then I can add to it as I go."

"I hope you're making enough for all the work you're doing," Nick commented.

"I believe I am. And, Kate, we need to talk about the rent I should pay you."

"Absolutely not. You help around here, and that's enough." Kate beamed at Abby, as if that was the end of the discussion.

"Kate, I love living here with you, and it's good for Robbie, but I have to pay rent. It's only fair to you. Keep the money and spend it on yourself. You can get a manicure, or have your hair done, or go into town for lunch. Do things that you enjoy."

"Oh, I don't think— Well, maybe some small amount would be reasonable, don't you think, Nick?"

"No." Suddenly, as if he'd had enough of this discussion, his demeanor changed. His lips tightened to a line, his eyes squinted. He was, Abby knew, trying to keep his anger in check. "Abby will not be paying any rent. I owe her for the last five years. Now it's only fair that she lives here free for the next five years."

But she refused his charity. "You're being ridiculous, Nick. I should—"

"That's the way it's going to be, Abby. My way." Losing the battle with himself, he advanced on her, his eyes flaring. "If you don't agree, you can move out." He stepped away but spun back, his words even sharper this time. "And I won't let you take Robbie with you."

CHAPTER SIX

"Nick, you're impossible!" Abby followed him as he stormed to the door. After all, this was her son he was talking about. "You can't tell me—"

The door slammed in front of her, making any further objection moot. Instead Abby banged a fist on the door frame.

Kate stepped up behind her, putting a consoling hand on her shoulder. "Come on, Abby. Let's have a cup of coffee. We can talk."

When they sat with their steaming mugs, Kate said, "We can keep this just between us girls. I know you have your pride, Abby, so I'm willing to accept rent from you. I know you won't feel comfortable living here any other way. But no more than a hundred a month."

Abby smiled. "Thanks for understanding, Kate. But I need to pay you more than that."

"Why? Like Nick said, he should've been paying child support all those years, and you've subletted your apartment to Julie when she couldn't find anything. You're family, honey, even if Nick didn't marry you."

"Oh, Kate, you're being too sweet to me."

Kate patted her hand. "Now, get busy writing those recipes. And maybe you can make me a copy of them, too. Brad was raving about the chicken casserole he ate for lunch today."

"Sure. And I've got a green enchilada recipe that he'll like, too. In fact, I can make it for dinner tonight if you'd like."

"I don't think you should have to cook after working all day."

"You've got to let me do some things for you if we're going to agree on the rent you'll take. I'll make dinner tonight and see if you like that recipe. Oh, and I've promised Robbie he can have his new friend Johnny Crawford over to play after school one day. Will that be okay?"

"Of course, whenever you want. Johnny is a nice boy."

"Good. I'll call his mother tonight and set up a date."

For the rest of the afternoon Abby worked on the recipes for the Rolodex while Kate made a chocolate cake for dessert. An hour before dinner, Abby got up and made the green enchilada recipe, while Kate observed. Then she set the table for dinner.

Matt and Jason had come in from school and started on their homework. Robbie pretended he had homework, too, sitting beside Matt.

Abby hoped Matt didn't get irritated by Robbie's behavior. But the boy was being patient and encouraging Robbie to do his "homework" as if it were real.

Just as they were putting dinner on the table, they

heard a car drive up. Kate hurried to the window over the kitchen sink. "Oh, my, there's Patricia."

"I'm sure I made enough for her, too," Abby said, trying to be gracious.

"I know, but dinner isn't much fun when she comes."

"Who's here?" Jason asked as he entered the kitchen.

"Patricia," Abby said.

The boy made a face and asked if he could take his meal in front of the television.

"Absolutely not," Kate hurried to say. "Go see if your brothers have come into the barn yet. You need to tell Nick that Patricia is here."

Jason nodded and headed for the back door. When he opened it, he had to step back and let Patricia in.

"Good afternoon, Jason," she said, as if attending a social tea. The boy nodded and went on his way.

Ever the polite hostess, Kate greeted her.

"Hello, Patricia. Nick's not in yet, but he'll be here soon. Won't you come in?"

"Thank you. Oh, my, I didn't realize I was coming at dinnertime. I don't want to be a bother."

"There's plenty of food if you'll join us," Kate said.

"Well, of course, that's up to Nick. We might want to take our meal in private."

"Nick knows he'll take his dinner at the table if he wants to eat," Kate returned with a smile and set another place at the table.

Abby had made two casserole dishes of the green enchiladas. She put the first one on the table, leaving the other in the oven until it was needed.

Kate had heated up some green beans and fixed a

salad. She began pouring tea, and Abby moved to help her, taking the glasses to the table. She also stepped to the door to call Matt and Robbie to dinner.

Patricia, of course, sat down at the table and didn't offer to do anything.

They could hear the three guys coming in from the barn. When they entered, Patricia popped up to greet Nick, but hesitated when she saw him dirty and sweaty from a hard afternoon's work. Along with his brothers he went to wash up.

Patricia promptly sat back down again.

Matt and Robbie came in to the kitchen, Robbie carrying the picture he'd been drawing of his family. He showed it to both Abby and Kate, pointing out everyone in the family.

"Where am I in the picture?" Patricia asked.

Robbie looked at his mother, panic in his eyes.

"I'm afraid Robbie has so many new people in his family, he might've forgotten to draw in future members," Abby said with an apologetic smile.

"He'll soon learn!" Patricia said stridently.

Robbie pressed against his mother's legs, staring at the woman who scared him.

"What's wrong, Robbie?" Nick asked as he came into the room.

Robbie ran to his father's outstretched arms and whispered something to him. He turned to stare at Patricia. "What did you say to my son?"

"He didn't draw my picture, but he drew everyone else. He doesn't think I'm part of the family!"

"I don't think that's a major catastrophe, Patricia."

"Come sit down, everyone, before the food gets cold." Kate motioned for her other sons to take their places.

Patricia stood and moved to Nick's side, whispering to him.

"No, Patricia. We eat at the table with everyone."

Dinner was different that night. Patricia criticized anything she thought Abby had made. Abby did her best to ignore the woman's words.

"Hey, Abby's come a long way. The first meal she cooked for me was franks and beans over a campfire. Remember, Abby?" Nick asked, a big grin on his face.

"I remember," Abby said softly, avoiding eye contact with Nick. They'd taken a ride out to the creek that day and then spread out a blanket. With his kisses, Nick had lit a fire in her long before he ignited the campfire. Later she'd roasted the franks while he'd wrapped his arms around her in the early evening coolness.

She'd never forget that day. It was when she realized she loved Nick.

"I don't like picnics," Patricia announced. "They're too messy!"

Abby looked at Nick, saying nothing. But in an instant she realized she'd made a mistake. He was looking at her, his eyes smoldering, remembering.

"Too bad," he muttered. "Picnics are great."

"I could do much better than a picnic," Patricia announced.

No one said anything.

Patricia tried again. "I could cook dinner for—for everyone on Saturday. I'd have enough time then."

"That's a lovely idea, Patricia," Kate said. "We accept."

Everyone stared at Kate.

"It will be a treat to have such elegant cooking," Kate said, smiling at Patricia.

"I'm glad someone appreciates my style of cooking." She sent a look Nick's way. "Did you hear, Nick? I'm going to cook for you on Saturday."

"Okay, if that's what you want to do. I've got to take Robbie to town on Saturday to buy him some cowboy boots, but we'll both be back for dinner."

"But surely you can buy him boots another day. I expect you to keep me company while I cook."

"We'll be back by four, I imagine. It shouldn't take much longer than that for you to get started. Besides, I don't keep Mom or Abby company while they fix dinner."

"But I can't be expected to cook so much by myself!"

"But they do it every day," Nick said, shrugging his shoulders.

"Fine! I'll be here at nine o'clock, Kate. You'll be ready for me then?"

"Of course." Kate sent an amused look at her son before she got up from the table. "I'll get the dessert." She brought out the chocolate cake she'd made, and Abby brought out the plates and forks.

As everyone expected, Patricia declined dessert, but she was the only one. Everyone else enjoyed the rich chocolate cake.

Then, without any expression of appreciation, Patricia excused herself and demanded that Nick at least see her to her car. Which, of course, meant she didn't offer to help with the cleanup.

But Nick resisted, "Aren't you going to help clean up?"

"Why, no, I'm not. I thought the rule was whoever cooks takes care of the cleanup."

Kate and Abby shared a look, which meant they could walk away on Saturday night, after eating the elegant meal Patricia was sure to prepare.

Neither of them protested at Patricia's words, so Nick stood to escort his fiancée to her car.

"Good thing it's Jason and Brad's turn to clean up tonight, isn't it?" Matt asked.

"Yes, dear, it is," Kate agreed. "Abby, you go ahead and give Robbie his bath. You'll need to get in bed early this evening."

"Okay. Come on, Robbie. Time for your bath."

"Okay, but I don't like it when that lady comes to dinner," Robbie muttered.

"That is your father's choice, sweetie." She led her son out of the kitchen just as Nick came in.

"That was fast," Brad said in surprise.

"Yeah. Where's Robbie?"

"Abby took him to bathe before putting him to bed," Brad answered.

"I've got to go talk to him."

"Nick, he didn't do anything wrong," Matt hurriedly said.

"Thanks for standing up for him, Matt, but I don't think he did anything wrong, either. I'm just going to reassure him about that."

"Oh, good."

Nick patted Matt on the back. "Yeah, good."

Then he headed down the hall to the bathroom Abby

used to bathe his son. He knocked on the door. Abby cracked it open and stared at him. "Yes?"

"I need to see Robbie for a few minutes," he said with a smile.

"He's taking his bath right now. I don't think—"

"There's no need to protect him, Mama Bear. I wanted to reassure him that Patricia was wrong."

"Oh. Just a minute." She turned away from the door and said something to Robbie. Then she opened the door to let him in.

"You can go, if you want. I'll keep an eye on him," Nick offered.

"No, thank you." She stood there with her arms crossed over her chest.

"You don't trust me?" Nick asked, a touch of outrage in his voice.

"Why should I?" she asked.

He didn't have an answer for her, so he turned around to talk to Robbie. "I just wanted to tell you that you didn't do anything wrong, not including Patricia in your family picture, buddy. She's not part of the family yet."

"Is she going to be part of our family?"

"I've asked her to marry me," Nick said matter-of-factly.

"So she's going to be my mommy?" Robbie asked in rising horror.

"No, sweetie," Abby said hurriedly. "I will still be your mommy. Patricia will be your stepmother, but I doubt that she'll want you to call her that."

"What will I call her?"

Abby looked at Nick for the answer.

"She'll probably want you to call her Patricia," Nick decided.

"Or Mrs. Logan," Abby offered.

"Come on, Abby, she's not that bad," Nick argued.

"We'll see." She turned back to Robbie. "The point is, sweetie, that I'm your mommy. For all time."

"Okay. I like that, Mommy."

"Me, too. Now let's wash your hair," she suggested, and let him lay back on her hand so she could get his hair wet.

"Do you do that every night?" Nick asked.

"Pretty much."

"Don't you wash your hair, Daddy?" Robbie asked.

"Of course I do. I just wondered in case I needed to give you your bath."

"Why wouldn't Mommy be here to give me my bath?"

"I will be, honey, don't worry."

"But you could get sick. And I would fill in for you, like I am in the mornings. We did just fine this morning, didn't we, Robbie?"

"Yeah, Mommy. Daddy helped me brush my teeth."

"I'm glad. I hope you minded him."

"He did," Nick said.

After rinsing her son's hair, she let him sit up. She stood and took a towel and handed it to him. "Dry yourself off. I'll go get your clothes."

"You can just give them to me. Robbie needs to learn to dress himself."

Abby looked at Nick. Finally she nodded.

"Why didn't you want Mommy to dress me?"

"You're almost five now. You need to start dressing

yourself, or having me help you. After all, Mommy is a girl."

"Okay," Robbie agreed, not sure he understood, but willing to trust his dad.

When they emerged from the bathroom, Robbie's pajamas in place, Abby told him to go say good-night to his grandmother. He ran down the hallway.

"Don't you think you're starting him a little early about dressing himself?"

"No, I don't. He's almost five. When is his birthday?"

"About five months away. February 26."

"He looks as big as the kindergartners now."

"I know. He gets that from you."

Nick nodded but he couldn't help the proud grin that split his face. "Abby," he added, his expression suddenly serious, "I just want to thank you again for Robbie. You had him on your own, and you never asked for help."

"I also didn't tell you about him. Remember?"

"I remember. But I've decided I don't blame you for that. I guess I didn't leave you many options."

She'd been picking up the bathroom. Now she turned to stare at him. "Why are you saying all this?"

"Because I realize it wasn't easy on you. I just want you to know I appreciate what you did."

"I didn't do it for you. I did it for me, and for my baby."

"Okay. But if you ever need anything, any help, let me know, okay?"

Abby couldn't help it. The words slipped out. "I don't think your new wife will take kindly to that idea. Maybe you'd better check with her first."

Nick's stance changed. He stood taller and crossed

GET FREE BOOKS and FREE GIFTS WHEN YOU PLAY THE...

Lucky 7

SLOT MACHINE GAME!

Just scratch off the silver box with a coin. Then check below to see the gifts you get!

YES!
I have scratched off the silver box. Please send me the 2 free Harlequin Romance® books and 2 free gifts for which I qualify. I understand I am under no obligation to purchase any books, as explained on the back of this card.

316 HDL ELUM **116 HDL EL2A**

FIRST NAME	LAST NAME

ADDRESS

APT.#	CITY

STATE/PROV.	ZIP/POSTAL CODE

7	7	7	**Worth TWO FREE BOOKS plus 2 BONUS Mystery Gifts!**
🍒	🍒	🍒	**Worth TWO FREE BOOKS!**
♣	♣	♣	**Worth ONE FREE BOOK!**
🔔	🔔	🍒	**TRY AGAIN!**

www.eHarlequin.com

(H-HR-07/07)

Offer limited to one per household and not valid to current Harlequin Romance® subscribers.

DETACH AND MAIL CARD TODAY!

The Harlequin Reader Service® — Here's how it works:

Accepting your 2 free books and 2 free mystery gifts places you under no obligation to buy anything. You may keep the books and gifts and return the shipping statement marked "cancel". If you do not cancel, about a month later we'll send you 6 additional books and bill you just $3.57 each in the U.S. or $4.05 each in Canada, plus 25¢ shipping & handling per book and applicable taxes if any.* That's the complete price and — compared to cover prices of $4.25 each in the U.S. and $4.99 each in Canada — it's quite a bargain! You may cancel at any time, but if you choose to continue, every month we'll send you 6 more books, which you may either purchase at the discount price or return to us and cancel your subscription.

*Terms and prices subject to change without notice. Sales tax applicable in N.Y. Canadian residents will be charged applicable provincial taxes and GST. All orders subject to approval. Credit or debit balances in a customer's account(s) may be offset by any other outstanding balance owed by or to the customer. Please allow 4 to 6 weeks for delivery.

his arms on his chest. His voice was deeper when he asked, "You think my wife is going to run my life?"

Abby didn't want to have this conversation now, but she'd known all along it would come eventually. Still, she'd started it, so she had to finish it.

"I think she'll try, and I don't want to cause you any problems in your marriage. I've managed by myself for five years. I think I can manage another five years by myself."

"But there's no reason for you to. I can help you."

"No, you can't. You owe your allegiance to Patricia."

Robbie came running back down the hall and Abby caught her son in her arms. "Okay, say good-night to your dad."

Nick hugged his son but then he followed them into Robbie's bedroom and helped tuck him in.

Abby listened to Robbie's prayers and kissed him good-night, reminding him to mind his dad in the morning. Then she left the room, followed by Nick.

"Abby?" he called softly.

"I'm going to bed now, Nick. I need to get to sleep."

"I know. But you don't have to work for a while now, you know?"

"No, I don't know. Why does it bother you so much that I'm working at the café?"

"You got your degree so you wouldn't have to work there again. It's like you're going backward."

Her career hadn't turned out the way she'd once planned. But now she had Robbie to worry about, Robbie to place above all else. "Don't worry about where I'm going, Nick. I'll find my way."

"Can't we at least talk about it?"

"What's there to talk about?"

"I can take care of you and Robbie. That's my job."

"We've already talked about this, Nick. You've moved on with Patricia, and I've moved on, too."

"You had boyfriends?" he suddenly asked, a frown forming on his face. "Did Robbie have 'uncles'?"

She stiffened. That was one topic of conversation she swore never to have with Nick Logan. He didn't have to know that there was never anyone after him. Once Robbie was born, she'd never had time for any other relationships. Even if she'd wanted one.

"That's none of your business," she said succinctly.

"I think it might be. He's my son!"

"Nick, you weren't around. I took proper care of Robbie. That's all you need to know."

"So someone else was kissing you?" His gaze fastened on her lips.

Instantly Abby felt the sensation of one of his kisses. She shook her head, hoping to shake off that feeling.

Nick leaned closer and she could once again imagine his lips on hers. "So, no one kissed you?" His voice had gone lower, deeper.

"I didn't say that. And we need to end this discussion now." She entered her bedroom and firmly closed the door behind her.

Before she found it impossible to go to sleep.

Nick stood there staring at the closed door. What more could he say? She was right about Patricia. She wouldn't let him do anything for Abby. If he married her.

He'd blown it. He'd thought Abby was out of his life. His mother had been encouraging him to find a woman and start a family. She'd even suggested Patricia. She'd met her a couple of times, but she didn't know much about her. Just that she was a home ec teacher.

Kate had figured she'd have all the skills needed for a rancher's wife. She was pretty enough, and they'd certainly shared some good times, enough that Nick had asked her to marry him. Once she'd accepted, though, her true personality had come out slowly but surely.

Seeing Abby again had made him realize Patricia's shortcomings. All the things he'd never recognized in her before.

Now, neither he nor his mother was too thrilled with his choice.

And he'd discovered Abby again, with his son.

Life had certainly turned around.

He wasn't sure what to do now. Stay the course he'd chosen? Or return to his old dreams?

Time was ticking, and he had to make a decision quickly.

Is there really a choice? asked an inner voice.

Truth time, Logan, he told himself.

Not really.

Going back to the kitchen, he found the room empty, everything cleaned and put away. He poured himself a cup of leftover coffee and sat down at the table.

He'd been there several minutes when his mother came to the door. "You okay?"

"Sure, Mom. I'm just doing some thinking."

"Need some company?"

"No. I've got some decisions to make."

Kate Logan was a woman of insight. And wisdom. This time her advice was succinct. "Don't choose the one that will make you miserable the rest of your life." Then she turned and walked away.

CHAPTER SEVEN

THE line at the café was out the door by the time they opened for business the next morning.

Abby already felt at home, and George, too, seemed to be more optimistic now that the patrons were back to the café.

Abby ran herself ragged waiting on all the tables. By eight o'clock, juggling four plates of short stacks, she told George, "We're going to need another worker for the breakfast rush."

"Yeah. I know someone I can call."

Twenty minutes later, Kate showed up at the café.

"What are you doing here?" Abby asked when Kate came in.

"I'm helping out. Where's another apron?"

"Behind the counter. I can't believe it!"

"I told George I could help him out in a rush. It's not like I have kids at home."

When Abby left at two, she was completely exhausted. But seeing Robbie gave her a second wind. She picked up her son and brought him home for a snack. After they played for a while, Robbie went to watch TV and Abby jotted some more recipes for George. She was still working when Nick came in.

"What are you doing in so early?" she asked.

"We didn't take canteens with us. I thought I'd get us a couple of drinks. Where's Mom?"

"I haven't checked, but I think she's taking a nap."

Nick gave her a strange look. Then he turned and went down the hall to his mother's bedroom. Abby got out a couple of cold bottles of water and set them out for Nick.

"Thanks," he said as he entered the kitchen and saw the drinks. "Mom is asleep."

"Yes, she came in and helped at the café this morning."

"Did you ask her to come to work?" Nick asked, a threatening look on his face.

"Of course I didn't! But even if I did, your mother could refuse. In fact, George called her without telling me."

"I don't like you using Mom. She's been very nice to you since you've come back."

"I know that! And I'm not lying to you!" Abby protested.

"No, she's not," another voice said, and they both whirled around to stare at Kate.

"What's wrong with you, Nick? If I decide to work at the café for a few days, I'm not skipping your meals. How dare you accuse Abby of thinking she can use me!"

"Mom, I just wanted to protect you. You already have a job."

"I get to make my choices. George is an old friend.

He called and told me he couldn't manage this morning without help. When I got there, people were standing outside, waiting to get in!"

"They were?"

Abby said nothing. She was busy at the counter and was ignoring Nick.

"But, Mom, you don't have to work at the café. We have plenty of money!"

"Yes, dear, we do, but George needs help."

Nick gave up the fight. "Thanks for the water, Abby," he said and walked out of the kitchen.

Kate let out a deep breath. "I'm sorry, Abby. I should've told him at lunch, but I didn't see any need to inform him."

"It's okay, Kate, but maybe you shouldn't—"

"I most certainly will. I have a date in the morning!"

Abby almost fell over. "What are you talking about?"

"I met the new sheriff in town. He's a lovely man, and he seemed interested in me."

"Kate! That's exciting—and Nick is going to kill me."

"Why?"

"I don't think Nick plans for you to move away."

"I don't intend to move away. I just want to have a little fun. What's wrong with that?"

"Nothing," Abby said, moving over to hug Kate. "You've more than earned a little fun."

Kate poured herself a cup of coffee. When she sat down at the table, Abby moved over to sit with her. "Tell me about the sheriff."

* * *

Nick didn't like the idea of his mother working at the café, but, as she'd pointed out, he had no control over what she wanted to do. And he sure didn't want another argument with her or Abby.

When he reached his brother in the barn, he handed the second water bottle to him. "Mom's working in the café."

Brad looked up. "Why?"

"George called and asked her to help out because he was getting a lot more business than he and Abby could handle. They were lined up outside the café when Mom got there."

"Wow! George is really doing well."

"You mean, Abby is doing well."

"Well, that's probably true. She's a good cook."

"Yeah, she is."

"Strange, isn't it? Patricia is teaching cooking, but I don't think she can cook as well as Abby."

Nick glared at his brother. "She'll cook a good meal Saturday night."

"Yeah, with tiny portions. You're going to get really skinny, like Patricia, if you're not careful."

"Let's get to work so we can make it to the supper table," Nick advised tersely. He was already concerned about what he'd done to himself. And he hadn't found a way out of his mess yet, no matter how long he thought about it.

He'd been sure Abby had found happiness in Cheyenne.

Happiness was different for different people.

But he hadn't been honest with himself. He'd been

playing the role of a martyr, sure he was sacrificing his life for the good of his family.

When he'd realized Abby had had his son, had kept the secret from him, his anger had crashed through the martyrdom he'd been wrapping himself in. If his martyrdom wasn't doing anyone any good, why was he playing that role?

But he'd trapped himself in a future marriage with a woman who was going to extend his martyrdom for the rest of his life.

What did he do now?

When Abby went into work the next morning, she vowed to keep an eye on Kate. Nick's mother had been a widow for five years. A lot had changed on the dating scene since Kate had been in the game.

When Kate arrived at seven-fifteen, she'd slipped in and put on her apron and begun waiting on customers. Since Abby hadn't met the new sheriff, she didn't know what or who to look for, but as she delivered breakfast to four men in the front booth, she noticed Kate chatting with a man several tables over. The next time she passed by that same table, she took a good look at the handsome man sitting there.

There was a star on his shirt almost hidden by the light jacket he wore. Fit and trim, with short light hair, he looked like someone Nick would like, but she wasn't sure Nick would be able to see past his mother's involvement.

"Is that your sheriff at table four?" she asked when she met Kate at the kitchen door.

Kate smiled. "Yes. Isn't he handsome?"

"Yes, but what is Nick going to say?"

"I'm not concerned with Nick's opinion, and you shouldn't be, either. After all, you're not responsible for me."

"But, Kate, I don't think Nick will see it that way."

"Me, neither," Kate said, a big smile on her lips as she picked up the order she'd been waiting for and sailed off across the room.

Lord have mercy, Nick was going to kill her if his mom had an affair with the sheriff. He'd blame her!

She made it a point to meet the sheriff as he stood up to leave. "Welcome to town, Sheriff. I'm Abby Stafford."

"Glad to meet you, Abby. I'm Mike Dunleavy." He shook her hand. "Sydney Creek sure is a friendly town."

"Yes, it is. Are you used to small towns?"

"Not really. I was a cop in Kansas City, but I decided I needed a change."

"Well, we hope you like it here." Abby said, though she noticed the sheriff's gaze wavering toward Kate.

"I'm sure I will, thanks."

When he'd tipped his hat to Kate before leaving the café, Abby couldn't help but hope Nick would approve. His mother certainly deserved some happiness. She'd been tireless over the years, raising five sons and a daughter, helping her husband run the ranch and carrying on when he was gone.

Abby vowed to keep her mouth shut about Sheriff Dunleavy until she had to admit knowing something.

Maybe he just liked finding a friendly face at breakfast. Maybe he'd never ask Kate to go anywhere.

Maybe she was going crazy, Abby decided. Kate was a wonderful woman; she still had her figure and a vibrancy that one could feel just standing next to her. And if she wanted the sheriff to ask her out, Abby imagined she could convey that message quite easily.

Kate left right before lunch, and Abby a few hours later. When she went to pick up her son and his friend Johnny, the boys were excited about their play date. She gave them their snack and then they headed to the barn to play with the puppies, where they spent the rest of the afternoon.

The boys were a delight, and Abby thought about asking Johnny to stay for dinner. Until Nick came in from the barn.

"I think it might snow tonight."

Abby was taking no chances. She quickly rounded up Johnny and his brother to get them home.

By the time she got back home, Kate was in the kitchen, having put in the casserole for dinner. "Thanks for making dinner again, Abby, but you don't have to do that."

"It's kind of become second nature after working at the café. If it's okay with you, Kate."

She grinned. "It definitely works for me!"

"What works?" Nick asked, coming in the back door at the tail end of their conversation.

"Abby fixing dinner again."

"You see, Mom, the working is too much for you. I mean, you—"

A stubborn Kate put him in his place. "I'm not at retirement age yet, Nick Logan! And I certainly can help out when my neighbors need me!"

"Settle down, Mom," he said, putting an arm around her. "I'm just trying to take care of you like Dad would've done if he were alive."

"I appreciate that, son, but I can take care of myself."

Abby thought this conversation was slightly familiar. Hadn't she just had the same one with Nick herself?

Kate continued, "Oh, by the way, I'm going out Saturday night, so I won't be here for Patricia's dinner."

"Where are you going?"

"Out with a friend."

Abby stiffened, afraid of what was coming.

"Who?"

"Do I ask you who you're taking out?" Kate returned.

"Well, not now, but I usually tell you anyway. Who are you going out with?"

"The new sheriff, Mike Dunleavy. Have you met him?"

Abby knew the minute Nick realized his mother was actually going out on a date. "You're going out with a man?" he blustered.

Abby stepped between the pair. "Of course she is. There's no reason she shouldn't, is there?"

Nick look affronted. "Of course there is! She's my mother!"

"So I have to join a nunnery because I'm your mother?" Kate asked.

Abby tried a different approach, asking another Logan male who'd just entered the room. "Brad, you don't mind if your mother goes out for dinner on Saturday night, do you?"

"Nope. Good for you, Mom." Brad shot her a wink.

Nick looked incredulously at his brother. "What are you thinking, Brad?"

"That Mom deserves some fun."

"Well, yes, but—but with another man?" Nick sounded outraged.

"Nick, I don't think Mom's going to date the town drunk. Are you, Mom?"

"No, I'm going to dinner with the new sheriff, Mike Dunleavy."

"There you go, Nick. Not only will she have fun, but she'll also be absolutely safe. What more can you ask?"

Nick glared at his brother and took his seat at the table. "I don't think you understand what could happen!"

"You mean Mom might marry again? Is that what's upsetting you?"

"Yes! What would we do, then?"

"Let Patricia take over the household?" In an exaggerated gesture, Brad slapped the palm of his hand against his forehead. "Oh, you're right, that would be a disaster. I can't imagine her willing to do all the work Mom does."

Nick suddenly looked at his brother, his expression reflecting a stillness of spirit. "How true. Sorry, Mom, I didn't mean to try to sway you. I'm sure the sheriff is a nice man. I'll look forward to meeting him."

Abby and Kate exchanged questioning looks. Then Abby asked, "So, you don't mind if your mother has a date with the sheriff?"

"Not at all. I want my mother to enjoy life. Brad is

right. Mom will have fun and be safe. I can't ask for more than that."

"Okay," Abby agreed. "Well, call the others for dinner, would you, please? I think it's almost ready."

Brad began helping his mother set the table and Nick went to find Matt, Jason and Robbie.

Abby didn't know exactly why Nick had changed his reaction. Clearly something had struck him in the middle of his tirade. She was curious about what had changed for him, but she was happy for his mother.

Except, of course, it meant she would be left to deal with Patricia by herself. That gruesome thought would ruin Saturday for her, but she wouldn't have Kate give up her evening. Maybe she should find someone to go out with. But who would protect Robbie?

She considered her options. Over the last two days at the café several men had flirted with her and asked her out. She'd smiled away their invitations. Perhaps she could simply agree to dinner with one of them and make it for Saturday night, leaving Nick to take care of Robbie. He wanted to be responsible for his son.

But, of course, he'd have to deal with Patricia, too.

A plan began to formulate in her mind. Maybe that was something he needed to realize. The hard way.

CHAPTER EIGHT

THE next morning, as if she'd planned it, a couple of old friends from the high school came in for breakfast. Abby talked to both of them, finding it fun to renew their friendship. Both were married, but before they left, they asked if she could get away one evening so they could catch up each other.

"I'm free Saturday night," she suggested.

The two ladies looked at each other. Heather said, "That works for me. How about you, Lucy?"

"Sure, I can get away. And we can call Cindy. She can get a sitter. A lady's night out! It'll be fun."

"Great. Where will we go?"

"There's a restaurant I like in Pinedale," Lucy said. "It's worth the drive and we can talk on the way there."

"Terrific. I'll meet you here at six."

Robbie didn't think it was too terrific. He groaned when he told her, after she picked him up at school. "But that's when that mean lady is coming. I don't like her."

"Your daddy will be with you," she said. Above all, she trusted Nick not to let Patricia be unkind to their son, or she wouldn't be leaving him.

It had snowed some last night and had turned icy, so Abby made Robbie play inside after school.

"I wish I had a Nintendo game. That would make it easy to stay inside."

"I can't afford to get you one right now, Robbie. Maybe for Christmas, okay? You know, just because we moved in with your dad doesn't mean we can have whatever we want, honey."

Abby kept the boy busy for the rest of the afternoon, looking forward to Nick coming in for dinner.

When she heard the kitchen door open, she went to him. "I wanted to tell you, Nick, I won't be here Saturday night, either. You should let Patricia know so she won't prepare too much food."

Nick looked like a hunting dog that'd just picked up a scent. "What do you mean?"

She looked at him in exaggerated surprise. "You didn't understand what I said? I said I wouldn't be here for dinner on Saturday night. I'm going out."

"Who with?" he asked tersely.

She stared at him, unable to figure out what was going on.

Fortunately Brad intervened. "He wants to know who you've got a date with," he said with a smile. "It seems my brother doesn't like to share his women."

"I am not his woman. His woman will be here cooking dinner." Fighting a blush, she looked at Nick. "And I'm assuming you can take care of Robbie, right?"

"Yes, I can, but you didn't answer my question."

"I'm going out with some friends I haven't seen since high school. We're going to gossip all evening. Is that a problem?"

"All women?"

"Yes."

"Then yeah, I can take care of Robbie."

"You won't let Patricia lose her temper, will you?"

"Of course not. Jason, Brad, will you two be here for dinner?"

Brad nodded and Jason reluctantly agreed.

"Then, there will be us five guys and Patricia."

"She'll be the only female," Abby remarked. "I'm sure she'll like that."

Kate chose the right minute to put the casserole on the table, avoiding any fallout from Abby's comment.

Brad drew a deep breath. "This looks really good, Mom."

"I didn't make it. It's another of Abby's recipes."

After the blessing, Nick served himself and took his first bite. "This is really good, Abby."

"Wait until you have a piece of pie," Matt added. "She gave us a taste for snack this afternoon."

Nick turned to her. "You baked pies, too?"

She nodded. "Last night. I—I couldn't sleep."

"You're getting an awful lot of work done," he said slowly. "I think you might be spoiling us."

"You're giving me and Robbie a place to live. I'm just grateful."

She ducked her head and began eating, but not before she caught the strange look Nick gave her. She felt his eyes on her all through dinner and suddenly Abby wasn't remotely hungry.

Not for food, anyway.

* * *

Nick was in a good mood. It was Saturday and he had big plans for the day. He waited until Abby offered to help Patricia in the kitchen and had been soundly rejected. Then he grabbed Abby's arm and drew her outside.

"What are you doing?" she asked.

"I'm taking you into town with me and Robbie. I may need your help fitting him."

"I don't think so. He wears normal sizes."

"I know, but boots fit differently. Come with us."

"Please, Mommy?" Robbie asked.

"All right, sweetie, we can do that."

Once they got to Sydney Creek, Nick led them to the general store and told the storekeeper he needed to buy boots for his family.

Abby whirled to look at Nick. "You mean for your son."

"And his momma," Nick said with a grin. "They're both living on the ranch, and they have to have the right clothes."

The man gave Abby a curious look and she blushed. But Nick didn't bother with an explanation. He ushered them to the boot section.

Half an hour later, both Robbie and Abby were dressed in new jeans and boots, as well as a hat. Abby had wanted to pay for her own things, but Nick told the shopkeeper to charge his account.

"Nick, you can't do that," she protested.

"Sure, I can. Now we're going riding."

Robbie saw nothing wrong with his father's decision. He couldn't wait to ride a horse.

"Nick, what are you doing? Patricia is going to be furious!"

Nick grinned at Abby. "My household has to be prepared to ride. We may need help if a bad snow comes."

"Is a bad snowstorm coming?" Abby asked.

"You never can tell. It's the season. Besides, Robbie needs some instruction. How about you? Have you ridden recently?"

"No. So I probably wouldn't be of much use."

Nick ignored her protests. "Robbie, I got you a small horse to ride. You'll like him."

"Isn't he too little to ride alone?" Abby asked, concern in her voice.

"Only because you kept him in the city. I was riding when I was three. Don't worry. This horse is tame. He has a companion horse for you."

"A what?"

"A horse that keeps him calm. She's a bay mare. You'll like her."

By then, they were back at the ranch. Nick led them directly to a back corral and introduced them to their mounts. Abby knew enough about horses to recognize the quality of the beautiful mare Nick intended for her.

He put Robbie up on his horse and led him around the corral, walking at his side. Abby couldn't help but notice how gentle he was with their son. And how handsome he looked in his cowboy hat and jeans. The last five years had only made Nick more gorgeous.

Robbie giggled and cheered, enjoying his time in the

saddle, till Nick called Brad to take Robbie in the house for a rest.

Then Nick led Abby's horse to her side. "Now it's your turn. I have to see if you still know how to ride."

"Nick, you can't take me for a ride while Patricia is cooking dinner for you."

"Sure I can. You offered to help, didn't you?"

"Yes, but—"

"Up you go," he said without waiting for her say-so. She sat in the saddle and away they went.

They rode for an hour, following a trail all the way to the creek. Alongside her, Nick talked about life on the ranch, asked questions about Robbie's childhood, and for the first time since she'd arrived at the Logan ranch Abby felt they truly connected. They talked and laughed and she couldn't remember a better time.

They stopped at the creek to let the horses drink, and memories of their time here so many years ago assailed her. Suddenly she was young again and in love.

Nick leaned against a tree trunk in a casual pose, but she felt tense. She could almost feel his kisses against her mouth, his arms around her waist holding her tight. It felt like yesterday when they were a couple in love.

As much as he tried to hide it, she knew he remembered those times, too. She could see it in his eyes.

Neither of them spoke of it, though. Instead they mounted up and returned to the corral.

When she dismounted, Abby thanked him for the ride. "I've got to go get ready for tonight, Nick, but the ride was fun."

"Abby—" He stopped then, and just looked at her, his expression unreadable.

For a moment Abby had the feeling he was about to say something really important, and back at the creek he'd looked like he was about to touch her. But he'd left her hoping then, and now he simply tipped his hat and let her walk away.

The kitchen was a mess by the time Nick came home around six o'clock with Robbie and Matt. He'd spent the rest of the day with them in town, where he'd bought Robbie a Nintendo game. Now he was looking forward to teaching him how to play, something he hadn't done since college.

He couldn't imagine what Patricia had been cooking since nine that morning. She was such a perfectionist. She'd used every pot his mother owned and had rearranged everything in the kitchen to her liking. That's the way she was.

When the three of them shut the back door, Patricia screamed at them. "You've ruined my soufflé! It mustn't be disturbed! You could've come in the front door!"

"How were we supposed to know?" Nick asked.

"Keep your voice down! Here I am slaving in the kitchen all day, and you're just running around playing! The least you could do was offer to help!"

"Abby offered to help you this morning. You turned her down quick enough, so why should I offer? I wouldn't be nearly as handy. Besides, I promised to take Robbie to get boots. And I got him a Nintendo, too."

"What a waste of money!"

Nick stiffened. "I don't believe you have any right to tell me how to spend *my* money! And especially not how to raise *my* son!"

"I don't see why it's not my business! We're going to be married. I have the right to complain when you're wasting our money."

"I don't expect *anyone* to concern themselves with *my* money!"

"When we're married, we will share *your* money, and you can count on that!"

"And you'll share your money, too?" he asked.

Patricia recoiled. "Well, no. If I choose to work, of course that money will be mine!"

"Wrong!"

"Nick, you're being ridiculous. Of course I'll keep my money for—for personal things."

"Then I'll keep mine for my personal things!"

She turned back to her preparations. "I can't talk to you about this right now. We'll discuss this later, after dinner."

"While we're cleaning up?"

Patricia jerked around. "What did you say?"

"I said we can talk while we're cleaning up."

"I'm not doing the cleaning up. I cooked all day."

"But the other night you said the cook does the cleaning. Well, tonight it's your mess, isn't it?" He gave her a smug look.

"I suppose if you help me tonight, I can, but we'll have to have a maid when we're married."

"I'm not having a maid!"

"Then your mother will have to do it," Patricia said, sneering at him.

"Let me get this straight. You intend to work and keep your money for yourself, but you expect someone else to do the housework? I don't think so."

"You're not poor, Nick. You can afford some help if your mother won't do the grunt work."

"Daddy," Robbie said, interrupting the fight, "can me and Matt take the Nintendo into the den and open it up?"

"Yes, son, I'll be there in just a minute."

After Robbie left the kitchen with Matt, Nick turned back to Patricia. "Save me some time after dinner." He started for the door. "We have to talk."

When Abby pulled up outside the house that night, she saw the kitchen light still on. Good. She was dying to find out how Kate's date went. And she'd have to admit she wanted to hear how Patricia's famous dinner went.

She slipped in the back door, never expecting to find Nick at the kitchen sink, apparently cleaning up.

"Hi, Nick," she said softly. "How was dinner?"

"A disaster," he said calmly, turning around.

"Why? Wasn't Patricia a good cook?"

"The food tasted good, as it should since she worked on it all day. But she was constantly criticizing our table manners and lecturing us on how and what we should eat. Everyone, except Patricia, was miserable."

"I'm sorry. She wasn't mean to Robbie, was she?"

"A couple of times, but I set her straight."

Abby didn't even want to think about what the woman had said to her son. "I think Robbie and I should move before you get married."

"You're not going anywhere. I said I set her straight."

"Some people can't be set straight. Patricia is one of them."

"You think so?"

"Yes. Where's Kate? Has she already gone to bed?"

Nick's face turned grim. "No. She hasn't come home yet!"

"Well, it's only ten-thirty. I'm sure she'll be in soon."

"I'm going to wait up for her."

"Why? Are you worried about her?"

"Maybe."

"Nick, she's with a policeman!"

"I don't know that. They had trouble getting someone with experience to take the sheriff job."

"He told me he'd been a cop in Kansas City."

"Why would a guy give up that job to come to Sydney Creek? I bet he was getting double what he gets here. There must be something wrong with him."

"Just because your romance isn't going well is no reason to spoil Kate's," Abby said.

She went to the refrigerator to get a glass of water. When she turned, suddenly, Nick was there, just inches from her.

"Wh-what do you want?" she asked, backing up the half-inch between her and the counter.

"I'm tired of people telling me what I can and can't do! And I'm not even marrying you!"

"No, you're not, so just back away. I can have an opinion without being married to you!"

Instead of backing away, Nick lowered his head as if he were going to kiss her. In a panic, Abby spilled the glass of water down the front of him.

"Dammit!" he yelled, jumping back as the cold water hit him. "Why did you do that?"

"I—I— You frightened me!"

"I did no such thing! I've been angrier than that with you before and you've never doused me with water then."

"I had it in my hand this time," she said, walking toward the door. She knew he was referring to a time at college when he'd seen a boy crowd her, trying to talk her into going out with him. She hadn't been about to agree, but he hadn't known that.

She had to get away from Nick now. "Be nice to Kate when—"

"Don't go. She's just pulled in."

Abby slowly came back into the room, but she kept the table between them.

"If I pour you a cup of coffee, are you going to spill it on me?"

"Not if you don't try to intimidate me."

"That wasn't what I was doing."

"It sure seemed like it to me."

He brought over two cups of coffee and set one down in front of her. Then he pulled out the chair next to her.

"I think you should move over a couple of chairs."

He glared at her, but then he moved over one chair. That was better than having him up against her.

The back door opened and both Kate and Mike came into the kitchen. "Oh! I didn't know anyone would still be up," Kate exclaimed.

"It's not that late," Nick said. "Abby just got in. I was asking her about her evening." He got up from his chair. "Hello, I'm Nick Logan, Kate's oldest."

"Why are you covered in…water?" Kate asked.

"We just had a little accident." Nick turned to his mother's date and extended his hand.

"I'm glad to meet you. I'm Mike Dunleavy. And you're—" He stopped when he looked closely at Abby. "You're Abby!"

"Yes, I am. Have a seat, Mike. I think Nick is going to get both of you a cup of coffee."

"Thanks, don't mind if I do. So you're Kate's daughter?" He was studying Abby as if trying to put together a puzzle.

"No. I'm—uh, I'm her grandson's mother."

Mike's gaze shifted to Nick, a question in his eyes.

"It's complicated. We broke up. When I found her a couple of weeks ago, she had my little boy, almost five years old. I insisted Robbie come back with me and— and Abby wouldn't leave him."

"Some people might call that kidnapping," Mike said slowly.

"No, Mike, they wouldn't," Abby said hurriedly. "I understood why Nick was angry, but he's been very good to me since we got back here. I live here with Kate and the other boys, too."

"So everything's all right? You're getting married?"

Kate said nothing and Nick looked horribly embarrassed.

"Um, no, Nick's already engaged to someone else."

"Who?"

Nick finally spoke. "Patricia Atwell."

"A teacher at the high school?"

"Yeah. You've met her?"

"Yeah. One of my deputies got on the wrong side of her temper when he had what she called the audacity to give her a ticket. She didn't think she should be fined just because she double-parked in front of a dress shop."

"Did you give in to her?" Nick asked.

"Of course not."

"Good for you." Nick grinned. "I'm glad I met you."

"Thanks."

"Did you see a movie tonight, Kate?" Abby asked, thinking a change of subject was advised.

"Yes, it was a lot of fun. But how did things go around here?"

"I just know Nick was cleaning up when I got home."

Nick explained, "That woman can't cook without using every pot in the house. By the time I fought with her and put Robbie to bed, I still had the kitchen to clean."

"Why didn't she clean it?" Kate asked.

"Because I insulted her, so, of course, she whisked out of here angry."

"It wouldn't surprise me to find that she'll be perfectly happy in the morning, as long as she's not facing a sink full of dishes."

"Come on, Mom, I don't think— Do you think so?"

Kate just nodded her head. "And don't think I'm abandoning my kitchen to her ever again, until I have to."

"You'll want to. She said someone else would have to do the cooking if she was going to keep working, which she intends to do, and pocketing her salary all for herself. She suggested I hire a maid unless you wanted the job."

Mike reached out and took Kate's clenched hands. "Don't worry, honey. I'll rescue you!"

"Yeah, so I can cook for you?"

"Why sure," he said with a big grin that had Kate smiling back at him.

"Not to worry, Sheriff. I'll take care of my mother."

"Right. Well, I'd better get out of the way so you all can get some sleep," Mike said, standing.

Kate immediately stood beside him. "I'll show you out."

When they walked to the back door, Abby stood and dragged Nick into the hallway, with him protesting all the way.

"What? Did you want to talk some more?"

"No. I was trying to give your mom some privacy."

"Why? Did you think— You thought he was going to kiss her?" Nick asked, outraged. He jerked his arm out of her hold and rushed back into the kitchen.

Abby heard Kate ask her son what was wrong.

"Abby thought the sheriff was going to kiss you good-night!"

"So?"

"Well, did he?"

"Yes, he did. Very nicely, thank you," Kate said and entered the hall where Abby was standing. She mouthed "thank you" and walked on down the hallway.

Nick came running after her.

"Nick, leave her alone. She's not your daughter. I guess I can be glad that Robbie is a boy!" she said with a smile.

"Damn right!" Nick muttered.

"So you've got double standards?"

"You bet I do."

CHAPTER NINE

THE next morning was Sunday, the only day that things slowed down on the ranch. Kate got up around seven to fix breakfast and the rest of them got up around eight to eat and be ready to leave for Sunday School.

Abby met Kate in the kitchen at seven and sat down with her to share some coffee. "Did you really like Mike?"

"Oh, yes. He's special. I never thought I'd find anyone else after Robert. But I think I have."

"Really? That's wonderful, Kate. Will you—will you marry him and move away?"

"No, I don't know that. I still have Matt and Jason to raise. Maybe we'll just date for a while. But I can't abandon my children."

"I think they could live with Nick and—and Patricia."

"I don't think anyone could live with Patricia! Not even Nick."

"But if Nick marries her, I'm sure he'll find a way to convince her to cooperate."

"He's dreaming if he thinks he can do that!" Kate said, just as Nick entered the kitchen.

"Who's dreaming about what?" he asked as he poured himself some coffee.

"You're dreaming if you think you're going to bring Patricia to heel so she won't upset everyone in the family." Kate pressed her lips together, not willing to take her words back.

"Come on, Mom, she'll come around."

"No, she won't. She's looking for a cushy spot where she can play a rich woman. And she's not going to change."

Abby sipped her coffee and kept her gaze lowered.

Nick sat down at the table. "What if you're right?"

"Then if you marry her, you'll be miserable."

Nick sighed and took a drink of coffee. "I'm going to talk to her."

"Good," Kate said.

Abby changed the subject. "They're organizing something at church this morning for a family in need. The Caldwells. Your mom talked to some people."

"Good for you, Mom! What are they thinking about doing?"

"Mrs. Caldwell is having some difficulties with her pregnancy, so we're raising money to hire a house-keeper until after the baby comes. That way she'll follow the doctor's order of bed rest."

"That's terrific!"

"Yes, it is. I think it will make everyone feel better taking care of the family," Abby said.

"I'll ask Patricia if she can do anything at school, maybe raise some money there, to help out."

Kate made a noise, and Nick looked at her. "Did you say something, Mom?"

"I said that was a dumb idea."

"Why?"

"Your fiancée isn't a kind person. She's not going to put forward any effort for anyone but herself."

"You could be wrong, Mom."

"Right," Kate said in a restrained tone.

Abby tried again to change the subject. "Um, I'll get started with breakfast. Are pancakes all right for everyone?"

"Yes, everyone will love your pancakes," Kate said, getting up to help her.

Nick sat there studying his cup of coffee, saying nothing else.

Abby whispered to Kate, "I think you may have overdone it. If he's determined to marry her, I don't think he'll give up now."

"I just wanted to make sure I finally told the truth. If he's fool enough to stay the course, I won't be here to help him out."

Abby started the pancakes when the others dragged in.

Robbie ran to her and wrapped his arms around her legs. "Good morning, Mommy. I missed you!"

"I missed you, too, sweetie. Did you make it all right last night?"

Robbie hung his head and didn't look up as he said, "Kind'a. But she didn't like me very much. She said I was a problem. I didn't mean to be a problem."

"I'm sure you didn't, sweetheart. I never found you

to be a problem," she said as she knelt down and hugged him. "Don't worry. Things will be all right."

"I don't want to go back to our old place!" Robbie said hurriedly.

"You're not!" Nick said.

"But—" Robbie began.

"Don't worry, sweetie. We'll work something out."

"What are you offering the boy?" Nick demanded.

"I only know that I'm not going to remain here when you marry Patricia, and neither will Robbie. It wouldn't be good for him to always think he's a problem."

"So just trust me for a day or two," Nick said abruptly. "You've only been here a couple of weeks."

"I'm not trying to put you in a difficult position, Nick, but I won't allow my son to be mistreated."

"Do you think I will?"

"I don't know."

"Just wait."

Frustrated and upset, Abby held her tongue. She didn't want to fight in front of Robbie. The boy had been upset enough. Forcing a smile on her lips, she turned to him. "Are you ready to eat, sweetie?"

"Yeah, I'm ready."

She took a big platter of pancakes to the table for him and Matt. As if on cue, Jason stumbled in to the table and flopped down in a chair. "I think Jason needs some coffee."

"I'll get it for him. Did you stay up too late?" Kate asked her son.

"Yeah. I was reading."

"Must be a good book," Kate said.

"It was lots better than hanging around with

Patricia," Jason said. Then he looked at his brother. "Sorry, Nick."

Brad walked in at that moment and greeted both women. "We really missed you two last night."

"You would've missed them more if you'd helped with the dishes." Nick took a bite of his plate of pancakes.

"I didn't think you two wanted company. You were hardly speaking to each other. I thought I'd be in the way."

"She left a couple of minutes later. She felt I was insulting her." Nick didn't even look up. He just kept eating.

"Sounds like a good excuse to me!" Brad said with a chuckle.

"Son, don't laugh at your brother's problems," Kate said softly.

"At least she's showing her true colors before the marriage. That's a warning, bro." Brad smiled at Abby as she set a plate of pancakes in front of him. "Thanks, Abby."

"You should've thanked Patricia last night," Nick said. "She was greatly offended that none of you thanked her." Nick looked at all his brothers.

"Hell, we were too interested in trying to get out of hearing range. She was so busy listing all our sins, she wouldn't have heard a thank you, and you know it, Nick!" Brad said. Then he looked at his mother. "Honest, Mom, it was the worst meal I've ever eaten, and I'm not talking about the food."

"Well, I'm glad the food was acceptable," Kate said.

"Yeah, it was acceptable, but both you and Abby can turn out as good a meal in half an hour and smile when you join us. I think that's more important."

"Thank you, Brad," Abby said.

Brad smiled and nodded as he took a bite of pancakes.

Nick pushed back from his plate, now empty, and stood. "Well, I guess I'd better take care of things before even the dogs start complaining about Patricia."

"What are you going to do?" Kate asked.

"I've got some ideas." He grabbed his hat off the rack by the door. "If I don't make it to church, I'll see all of you later."

The drive to Patricia's apartment seemed endless. Nick knew exactly what he had to do and couldn't wait to get it over with. He was dumping Patricia.

He'd finally accepted the fact that they were poorly matched. Not only did he not love her, but he also couldn't stand to be in the same room with her, much less the same bed.

He'd finally accepted the fact that the only woman he wanted in his bed had helped make breakfast this morning.

Abby.

He'd been in love with her for so long, he couldn't remember a time when he didn't love her. He never knew how hard it would be to have her around and not be able to touch her, to kiss her, to show her how he felt about her.

The more time he spent with Abby, the worse Patricia looked to him. And the more he tried to explain why their marriage wouldn't work out without mentioning Abby, the worse things had gotten.

But now he had the perfect plan. He'd make it clear

to Patricia that they were through, but then he was going to allow her to save face by letting her reject him. Part of him felt he owed her that. But she had to do it at once, or he would tell everyone the truth, that he didn't want her.

If she cooperated with him, then he would hold off asking Abby to marry him for at least a month. Maybe a month. He'd rather ask her sooner, but he was trying to be reasonable.

He'd called Patricia from his cell phone after he'd left the breakfast table to tell her he was coming over. Strangely enough, she'd sounded pleased. He would've thought last night would have upset her too much to see him today. It had certainly upset his family.

When Nick reached town, he pulled up to a two-story stone house on Elk Street. Patricia rented the upper apartment. He took a deep breath and knocked on her door.

Patricia opened the door, poking her head around it. "Come in," she said in a soft voice, one he supposed she thought was sexy. He did as she asked.

After she shut the door, she whirled around and smiled at him. She was dressed in a revealing black negligee.

"Uh, Patricia, I think you've gotten the wrong idea," Nick said, backing away from her reaching arms.

"Did you think I hadn't forgiven you for last night? I knew when you called this morning that you felt bad about the way you had acted."

"No, Patricia, I didn't," he said, keeping his distance.

Patricia stopped, the smile disappearing. "Surely you realize how rude you were! There can be no discussion about that, and I won't accept a repeat of such behavior."

"And I won't accept your behavior again. Mom said you're not taking over her kitchen, either."

"I didn't destroy anything!"

"How do you know? You certainly didn't clean up. I believe I was left to do that."

"That's because you insulted me."

"Whatever the reason, it's not going to happen again."

"Fine. I won't cook if you don't want me to. I'll be too tired after I teach all day, anyway."

"My point," Nick said grimly, "is that you won't be cooking for me or anyone else in the family because you and I aren't getting married." There, he'd said it.

"What? You can't do that to me! I've made plans!"

"I'm sure you have, but you'll have to make new plans that don't include me. I'm going to marry Abby."

"How dare you!" She pointed a manicured finger at him. "I'm going to sue you for everything you've got."

"On what basis? Because I think I can prove you didn't meet *my* expectations, either. And I'm offering you a chance to tell everyone you decided you dumped me. I won't say anything to Abby for a month. But that's the longest I'm giving you."

She scoffed. "I don't think she'll take you. Especially if she knows you slept with me!"

"We both know I didn't. And she'll believe me."

"You have a lot of faith in her, don't you? I bet she can't produce the dinner I did last night."

"She can do just as well in thirty minutes and she smiles while doing it," he returned, paraphrasing his brother's remarks. "You know what's wrong with you,

Patricia? You think you're always right. You need to entertain the possibility that you're not right all the time."

She still looked incredulous. "I can't believe you're breaking off our engagement!"

"I apologize, Patricia, but I didn't know about my son…or Abby when I agreed to get married, though you'll have to admit it was your idea. I made the assumption that you'd be a good rancher's wife. But if I were you, I'd look for a city man. You're better suited for that lifestyle."

"I don't care what you think!"

"Fine. Have we got a deal? One month to tell people we're not marrying before I say anything to Abby. And you get to keep your engagement ring." She'd insisted on a big diamond.

"Fine!" She tossed back her mane of hair.

"If you say anything nasty, the deal's off. You got that?"

"Of course," she said, her features frozen in a distasteful pout.

"I mean it," Nick said firmly. "Don't think I'll remain a gentleman if you try to play dirty."

"Just go, Nick Logan! I'm done with you."

On that point, he had to admit she was right.

As he left her apartment his face broke into a smile. He was going to be reunited with Abby. She was perfect for him and for his family. He couldn't wait to tell her. But he'd have to wait, at least a month.

He could do that. After all, he'd waited five years to find her and his son.

He was walking to his car, eager to get home, when he saw the sheriff crossing the street toward him.

"Morning, Mike. How are you this morning?"

"Fine. Got time for a cup of coffee?" he asked, gesturing to the café.

"Sure." They met on the sidewalk and crossed to the café.

"What are you doing in town on a Sunday morning?" Mike asked.

"I was having a conversation with Patricia."

"Oh, yes, your fiancée. I guess that's a good way to start the day."

"More than you'll ever know," Nick muttered. They entered the café and took the first booth.

"I thought it might be a good time for us to get better acquainted. I don't want you to think I'm not serious about your mother."

"You're serious? Already? You've only had one date."

"Nick, when you're my age, it doesn't take long to make up your mind. And your mother is the sweetest woman I've ever known. Why the men around here aren't chasing after her, I'll never know, but I'm glad they aren't."

"I'm not sure my mother would want to move as fast as you seem to be moving."

"Well now, I'm not telling you this because I want your help convincing your mother. I just thought I should give you a chance to learn a little more about me. You see, I was married for nineteen years to a wonderful woman. She died of breast cancer. I wasn't ready to look for anyone else, even though I had some chances."

"I'm sorry to hear that."

"That's why I decided to take the job here. I wanted a life that wasn't rushing away. The slower pace of a small town. I like it here and I hope to stay. More so now that I've met your mother."

"I see." Nick didn't know what else to say.

"Do you have any questions for me? Anything you want to know about me?"

"No, except my mother still has two younger boys at home, Matt and Jason. But it doesn't mean you'd have to take them if you and Mom decide— They can stay with me, whatever happens."

Mike shook his head. "Not going to happen. Whatever your mother decides, she'll have her children with her, and I wouldn't have it any other way." Mike paused before he said, "Your mom is real concerned about Miss Atwell."

"I think Patricia is changing her mind. But keep that under your hat. In fact, you could do me a favor."

"Sure."

"Just keep an ear to the ground and make sure she's not lying about my character. We have never slept together, whatever she says. I've agreed to let her announce our breakup. But she's not supposed to lie about me. If you hear something, let me know."

"Will do. And if you come up with other questions for me about me and your mom, I'd appreciate it if you asked me straight out."

Nick slid out of the booth and extended his hand. "You've got a deal, Mike."

Abby and Kate had just settled down in the pew, with Robbie between them, when Nick suddenly appeared and squeezed in the little bit of space that was left over, his arm extending along the back of the seat. Abby immediately asked Kate to scoot down a little, but Nick whispered in her ear, "I like it cozy."

Abby turned around to stare at him. Then she quickly slid down the bench so he had plenty of room. Robbie immediately wanted to sit between his mom and his dad, and Abby thought that was a good idea.

Nick kept his arm on the back of the seat, still touching her shoulder every time he moved, but she worked hard to ignore his touch. Nick's touch had always had an effect on her. That still held true.

After the final prayer, Nick stepped out into the aisle and held Robbie back so the ladies could go in front of them. That was something nice for Robbie to learn.

He was growing fast, but it was important for his manners to grow with him. Learning them from his dad made her life easier.

Once they were outside, Nick asked her if she'd ridden to church with his mother.

He was certainly acting strange today, she thought. "Yes, of course I did." There was no point in bringing more than one car for just the three of them. Jason and Matt had come with friends.

"Then why don't you ride home with me so I'll have some company."

"I don't think Patricia would like that."

"She can't control my behavior. We're friends, aren't we? Haven't we always been friends?"

"Yes, but— I think I'd better go with your mother. You take Robbie with you."

Nick was left staring as she crossed the lawn to his mother, who was visiting with neighbors. Then Abby bent down and whispered something to Robbie and he came running over to Nick.

"Hi, Daddy. Mommy said I get to ride with you!"

"Right, son. Let's go get in my truck and head home. We don't want to be too far from your mommy, do we?"

"Did Nick upset you?" Abby had barely sat beside her in the car before Kate asked the question.

"No. Not at all." Abby had never lied to Kate and felt bad about doing it now. She tried the truth. "He wanted me to ride home with him, but I just didn't think it was a good idea. After all, Patricia gets upset about ridiculous things. Even though Nick and I are friends, I don't think we should publicly get together."

"Hmm. That's interesting. That's the first time he's tried to get you alone. Right?"

"Yes, except when we went riding yesterday afternoon. But he didn't mean anything."

Kate took her eyes off the road long enough to shoot her a look. "You went riding?"

"He bought a mare for me when he bought a small horse for Robbie."

"Oh, I see!"

Abby felt the emotion rise like bile in her throat. She could no longer swallow it.

She looked at Kate and blurted, "I'm afraid I'm going to have to move out."

CHAPTER TEN

"WHAT'S wrong?" Kate asked, concern in her voice. "I thought everything was going well!"

"It's—it's just too difficult." Abby turned her gaze forward. "Think how hard it would be to live in the same house with Mike, but you can't touch him, you can't share your thoughts with him." She blinked back tears that stung her eyes. "Nick and I have got a history that can't be forgotten. No matter what he threatens to do about Robbie, I don't think Patricia will let him have Robbie with them. And it wouldn't be good for Robbie."

"I know," Kate said sadly. "I knew it would come to this, but I can't tell you how sad I am. I was hoping you'd be able to tempt Nick back to his old self. It's been terrible having the possibility of Patricia in our family."

"I know, Kate. I'm so sorry."

Kate patted her leg. "When will you move?"

"I'll have to find a place. I want to remain in Sydney Creek so Robbie can see Nick. But I'll miss you. I hope we can still be friends."

"You know we will, Abby. I made a mistake five years ago. That won't happen again."

"Thank you, Kate." Abby lost the battle with her tears, and now they slid down her cheeks.

"There's only the one apartment house in town. I don't think you'd be happy there. But I believe George has a second apartment over the café. He hasn't rented it out for a while, but he might to you."

"That would be perfect!"

"I don't know. I think it's just one bedroom."

"Robbie can have the bedroom and I'll get a sleeper sofa for the living room. We'll be fine," Abby said firmly, determined to believe what she was saying.

When they reached the house, Nick's truck was already parked there. Abby wiped away her tears and drew a deep breath. "Don't say anything about my decision. We'll just wait until I actually move out."

Kate looked at her. "But it might force him to wake up."

"I don't want a man who has to be woken up in order to want me and love me, Kate." She shook her head. "No, our time has passed. If it weren't for Robbie, I would just disappear. But Robbie ties me to him."

Kate nodded. "Okay, we'll do it your way."

They entered the house and heard Robbie squealing and giggling. They exchanged looks and followed the sound into the den, where Robbie and his father were playing Nintendo.

"Where did that come from?" Abby asked.

"Hi, Mommy. Daddy bought it for me yesterday. Isn't it neat? Do you want to play? Daddy will let you take his controller."

"No, thank you, Robbie, but I do need to talk to Daddy," Abby said with a direct look at Nick. "Maybe Grandma can play with you for a minute."

Abby turned and walked into the kitchen.

When Nick got there, she immediately asked, "Why did you buy him Nintendo?"

"Because he asked for it. What's the big deal?"

Abby took a deep breath. "You can't buy him things all the time. You already bought him boots and a hat, didn't you?"

"Well, yeah, but those were things he needed, not something he wanted." He tried to take her hand but she stepped back. "Come on, Abby. I just wanted to buy him something. I haven't been able to do anything like that for five years. Is that so bad?"

Much as she hated to admit it, she could see his point. "Okay," she conceded, "but don't buy him expensive things without talking to me. We don't want to spoil him."

Nick's face broke into a smile, the kind that always ignited a fire deep inside her. "Sure. We'll work together." He stepped toward her. "We were always so good together."

The innuendo wasn't lost on Abby. She got his meaning, and she moved away. Why was Nick doing this to her? Making things so difficult?

"I—I have to fix lunch," she stammered, fleeing across the room to open numerous cabinets, as if to appear busy. When Nick finally left the room, she slumped against the counter. It was clearer than ever now. She needed to get out of the house as soon as possible.

Without hesitation she grabbed the phone and dialed

the café. After a short exchange of pleasantries, she got to the point of her call. "George, I need to move to town and Kate said you have a second apartment over the café. Would you rent it to me?"

"Well, sure, if you want it, but it's a mess."

"Don't worry, George, I can clean it up. Thank you so much. Uh, I'll come into town this afternoon to start working on it. Is that okay?"

"Sure, that'll be fine. And, Abby, I used your recipes and the food turned out good."

"I'm glad, George."

When she hung up the phone, she leaned against the wall. She didn't want to leave the Logan ranch, but she had to. Her system couldn't take much more exposure to Nick. It had been okay in the beginning because Nick was mad at her. But for some reason now he wanted to be friends. Friends! How had she become his friend rather than his lover?

Stupid question!

She moved away from the phone and walked over to prepare lunch. Kate, having been relieved from the Nintendo controller by Nick, joined her. "I'd never seen that game before, but, you know, it's kind of fun. At least for a little while."

Abby gave a brief smile and kept working.

"What did you and Nick talk about?"

"I just warned him about buying too many expensive toys for Robbie. I don't want him to get spoiled."

Kate seemed to adopt Abby's solemn attitude, and nothing more was said.

After lunch, Abby asked Kate if she'd keep an eye on Robbie for the afternoon.

"Sure. Is everything all right?"

"I'm going into town to—to work on what we talked about earlier."

"Oh. Of course. Robbie is out playing with his puppy and Nick is with him. I'll keep an eye on him."

"Thank you, Kate." Dressed in jeans and an old sweatshirt, Abby drove to town. From what George had said, she would need to get down and dirty to make the place livable.

Fifteen minutes later, she realized George was right. The apartment was a disaster. Over the years George had stored old junk in the bedroom and rented the place as a studio. But after the last person moved out, George had done nothing with it. It was dirty, filled with cobwebs and junk left behind.

Abby fought back tears. Her life had come to this? To this pit of old and useless things! Then she gathered herself. She could clean it up and make it look better. There was nothing wrong with hard work.

She drew a deep breath and dug in with the broom she'd borrowed from George. Three hours later, she'd barely made a dent in the disaster she'd first seen, but she was exhausted.

She promised herself that she'd work on it after work the next day, and the day after that. However long it took, she'd create a home for her and Robbie.

"Where's Abby?" Nick asked as he and Robbie came in the house.

"She went into town for a little while. Have you had fun today, Robbie?"

"Yes, Grandma. We played with Baby. Daddy says maybe soon I can bring her to the house and she can even sleep with me!" Robbie's face glowed at the thought.

"That's nice, dear. We'll be ready for dinner in a few minutes."

"But where's Mommy? Is she going away again?" Robbie asked, a frown replacing his happy expression.

"Well, Mom?" Nick prodded.

"No, I don't expect— In fact, I think that's her car now," Kate said, moving to the kitchen window. "Yes, that's her."

Robbie ran outside, closely followed by Nick.

They both came to an abrupt halt when Abby got out of her car. "Mommy, what happened to you?" Robbie demanded, staring at her dirty clothes and her smudged face.

"I've been helping George with a project, sweetie. I'll look more like myself after I take a shower."

Nick was frowning at her. "What kind of project?"

"One I chose, Nick. Now, if you'll excuse me…" She pushed her way past Nick. He was glaring at her, but having him angry with her was better than him trying to be *friends*.

Nick returned to the kitchen. "Mom, you know what Abby was doing, don't you?"

"Yes."

"Then tell me."

"I can't. I promised her I wouldn't."

"But she's already working five days a week. She shouldn't have to do more."

"She gets to make her choices. Remember? The last time you made a decision for her, it didn't work out. Think about that."

"But I was only doing what—"

"Exactly!" Kate carried a bowl to the table.

"Then I'll go ask her what she's doing." He stomped out of the kitchen.

When he reached the bathroom where Abby was showering, he knocked on the door, but she didn't hear the knock. At least that's what he assumed. So he opened the door.

"Abby?"

She stuck her head around the curtain. When she saw Nick there, she screamed and reached for her towel. "What are you doing in here? Get out!"

"I want to know what you're doing!"

"I'll talk to you when I'm dressed! Go away, Nick!"

"Abby—"

"Get out!"

Nick stepped out of the bathroom only to find his mother ready to chew him out.

"What do you think you're doing?"

"I'm just trying to get the truth out of Abby!"

"Well, I think it's a little unfair to try to talk to her when she's taking a shower!"

"I'm sorry, Mom. I—I— She just makes me lose control."

"It's Abby who deserves your apology. For now, go back to the kitchen and reassure your son."

Once Nick had walked down the hall to the kitchen, Kate knocked on the door. "Abby? Are you okay?"

The door opened and Abby stood there, wrapped in a towel, her hair dripping. "I'm okay. Why did he... Oh, never mind. It doesn't matter. I'll be gone in a day or two."

"That soon? Are you sure you have to go?"

"Is there any doubt after Nick's behavior tonight?" Abby asked, looking directly at Kate.

"No, but I wish—" Kate shook her head in despair. "I came to tell you dinner is ready. Can you come eat?"

"I'll be right there."

When Kate walked into the kitchen, Nick immediately bombarded her with questions.

"Is she all right? Is she coming to dinner? What do I need to do?"

"She'll be in to pour the tea like she always—" She broke off, sudden tears filling her eyes. Another meal or two and Abby wouldn't be putting the tea on the table as she usually did. She, and Robbie, would be eating alone in their little apartment. The huge ranch house would feel empty without them. Clearing her throat, she said, "Nick, please take the tea glasses to the table."

Nick did as he was asked, just as Abby entered the kitchen and was greeted by everyone. Robbie jumped down from his chair and ran to greet his mother.

"Where did you go, Mommy? I missed you!"

"I had to go to town. Were you a good boy?"

"Yes! Daddy said so!" Robbie said with a big grin.

Abby's gaze flickered to Nick's and away. "I'm sorry I didn't get back in time to help with dinner, Kate."

"It's not a problem, Abby. You've done so much

around here, ever since you arrived. It's hard to believe it's only been a couple of weeks."

From the end of the table Brad looked at Abby. "Yeah, you blend in nicely with the family, Abby. It's a pleasure to have you around."

Abby kept her gaze on her plate, afraid that if she looked at the Logans, she'd burst into tears. After misunderstandings and five long years, she'd come to love them all. She cleared her throat and took her seat. "Thank you, Brad."

When she looked up to pass the platter of roast beef, she noticed Nick staring at her. The small smile on his face reached his eyes, making them dance. What was he so happy about? she thought.

Probably thinking she could stay and be the maid, as he'd told Kate Patricia had suggested. Well, he could think again!

Just then the phone rang.

Kate answered it. "Hi, Mike. Yes, of course." She turned around. "Nick, the phone is for you."

Nick looked surprised. "He asked to talk to me?" He got up from the table and crossed to the phone. "Hello?"

After a minute, the pleasant expression on his face tightened and his eyes darkened. "What! I'll be there in five minutes!"

Then he stormed out of the house without saying a word.

"I hope he wasn't going to town, 'cause that takes longer than five minutes," Brad said.

No one wanted to guess his destination.

* * *

Nick couldn't believe it.

Just that morning Patricia had agreed to his ban on trash-talking. He'd admit he really hadn't expected her to say nice things about him. But bashing him on the first day?

And it wasn't him she was attacking. It was Abby.

She was apparently labeling Abby as the town slut who was sleeping with him during his engagement. He wasn't going to tolerate that!

Mike had promised to wait at the café for him with the man who had passed on the gossip about Abby. When Nick entered the building, he saw the young man beside Mike, looking very uncomfortable.

Nick stepped forward and extended his hand. "Bill Lamb, I haven't seen you in a while."

"Look, Nick, I—I didn't mean to— I mean, I was just repeating what I heard and, I—"

"It's not smart to repeat something you don't know is true," Nick said conversationally. "Just who told you such nasty gossip?"

Bill swallowed hard. "Well, that's the thing, Nick. I wouldn't have repeated such a thing, except that I heard it directly from Patricia Atwell."

Nick stared at the man. "Directly from her? It's Sunday evening. Where were you that you picked up the latest gossip?"

"Here at the café! She came in and made a big production of tears and everything, telling us how she'd been wronged by that, uh, that other woman at your mother's."

"Bill, I thought you knew my mother."

"Why, a'course I do. Fine woman."

"And you think she would allow such carrying on under her roof?"

"I did think about that, but Patricia said the boy was yours and I figured that might account for it. There's also the fact that Patricia isn't a very likable woman. I thought maybe you got tired of her."

"I did, but I made the mistake of telling her face-to-face. She promised she would be a lady about it. Obviously she doesn't know the meaning of the word."

The man began to relax a bit now that he wasn't going to incur the wrath of Nick Logan. "I—I wouldn't have said anything. Give my apologies to your mother."

"Yes, I will, Bill."

After the man shuffled out of the café, Mike gestured to a booth. "Want to talk about it?"

"What I want to do is take her head off!" Nick muttered. "But I don't know what I can do…legally." Nick sat down in the booth opposite Mike.

"Well, since he got his words directly from your ex-fiancée, I think you've got a good case for suing for slander and character defamation. But I'm no lawyer."

"Neither am I. But is it possible to threaten her with it and not follow through?"

Mike grinned at him. "Anything's possible. And I could come along with you, to throw my weight around. Sometimes the badge intimidates 'em."

"Let's go."

When they crossed the street to Patricia's apartment, Nick banged on the door.

He heard Patricia sing out, as if she were in a good mood, "Who is it?"

"Nick!" he returned sharply.

Silence followed. Then she said, "Go away. I don't want to talk to you."

"So you prefer that we shout our business through the door so everyone in town can hear what happened?" Nick offered in a dire voice.

She yanked open the door and noticed Mike Dunleavy. "What's he doing here?"

"He's here in case I need him."

Patricia snorted. A quite unladylike gesture, Nick thought.

"What do you want, Nick?"

"I thought we had an agreement, Patricia. I would let you break up with me as long as you were nice about it."

"You said if I was nice about *you*. I didn't say anything to denigrate you," she said, her nose in the air.

"But you thought it would be all right to throw Abby beneath the wheels? I don't think so! How dare you tell such vicious lies about Abby!"

"I don't know they're lies. You've slept with her before!"

"Yes, more than five years ago. And never since. I was engaged to you."

"Until you broke it off! What did you expect me to do? To just accept your dismissal?"

"You should've accepted it. Now, I'll take you to court and prove that you were lying. I'm going to sue you for everything you've got."

"You're the one with the money, not me! Besides, you can't do that. It's not fair."

"Look, I left you with the engagement ring. You should've accepted what I said. You would've been as miserable as me if we'd married. There was no way you were going to get your way."

"I had every right to expect to marry you. If you sue me, I'll sue you in return for breach of promise."

"No court would uphold that. And even if it did, that doesn't give you the right to attack the woman I love."

She stuck her nose in the air. "Do what you will. I'm leaving town as soon as I can. I certainly don't want to hang around here."

"Good." He turned around, with Mike right behind him, and returned to the café.

George greeted them at the door, a towel over his arm and a ladle in his hand.

"So you're in love with Abby?"

CHAPTER ELEVEN

NICK could only stare at George. "Yes, I am. But how did you know?"

"One of my customers told me. They just heard you shouting about it to that strange woman who came in earlier. I told her just to get out of my café. She couldn't say bad things about Abby!"

"I'm glad you stood up for her," Nick said with a big grin.

"A'course I did. She's going to live here with me."

Those words brought Nick to a halt. "She's what?"

"She's cleaning out the second apartment upstairs so she can move in. What's wrong with—"

George didn't finish his thought because Nick was charging out of the café and around the back to the outside stairs that led to the second apartment. It wasn't locked, so he swung the door open.

It was easy to see how far Abby had gotten. And how hard she'd worked. But the place was still a mess. Abby would rather live here than at the ranch?

Obviously he had some work to do, to convince her to stay. Or maybe he shouldn't. Maybe he should let her move away and then court her. He probably owed her a courting.

He'd rather move straight to the loving, but he wasn't going to rush things this time. He wanted to be sure Abby was his bride. Forever.

He came back down the stairs, meeting Mike at the bottom of them.

"Abby's moving up there?" the sheriff asked.

"No, she's not going anywhere. That room's not fit for humans."

Nick stood there, thinking. "I'm not sure what to do, Mike. I want Abby. We should've been married five years ago, but I screwed up. How do I let her know I love her?"

"You mean other than just coming out and saying the words?" Mike asked. "Hmm, that's a tough one."

Nick began to pace. "I've got to figure out what to do."

"You could wait until tomorrow night and take her out on a nice date. I'll come help Kate baby-sit."

Nick noted the man's expression. "Yeah, I can tell you're dreading that!"

"Any time spent with Kate is great."

"Yeah. I feel the same way about Abby."

The two stood there in the moonlight grinning at each other.

Abby and Kate had cleaned the kitchen together, giving the boys a night off.

"I'm going to miss you so much," Kate said.

"I'm always glad to help."

"I'm not talking about your help, Abby. It's almost

like I have Julie back home. I'm not alone with a bunch of males. I have another woman to talk to, to share things with. I won't have that when you go."

She reached out and hugged Abby.

"Hey! Why are you hugging my mommy?" Robbie asked as he entered the kitchen, Brad right behind him.

Kate wiped her tears on her apron. "I—I was telling your mother how nice it is to have her here."

"I'm here, too," Robbie pointed out. His grandmother opened her arms and he flew into them.

Brad shot a questioning look at Abby, but she said nothing. He turned back to his mother. "Did you hear bad news from Nick?"

"No, we haven't heard anything," Kate managed to say.

"Are you all right, Mom?"

"Yes, dear, but I'm not too fond of change."

Again Brad looked at Abby.

Since she said nothing, he asked, "You mean Patricia coming?"

Kate poured cups of coffee all around, even a cup for Robbie with chocolate milk in his. They all sat down at the table. "That marriage is going to be the death of me," Kate finally said. "I refuse to share a house with her. But Nick is the oldest son. This house is big enough for all of us—unless one of us is Patricia."

"Yeah," Brad said. "I can't believe he proposed to her. I know she was being sweet and agreeable before he did, and I suppose he thought it would be good for all of us, but—"

"Brad, I'm moving out," Abby finally admitted.

"Robbie and I. We're going to live in town, over George's café. That will remove a lot of the irritants for Patricia."

"Yeah, but—"

"I know Nick's threatened a lot of things, but he's got to see how impossible it would be to remain here after he marries Patricia. It's not often the ex-girlfriend and the illegitimate child are part of the same family."

"Mommy, what are you saying?" Robbie asked in a small voice.

Abby bent down and hugged her child. "I mean, we are moving to an apartment over the café. I can walk you to school each day from there. And on weekends, you can probably come out and visit Grandma and your puppy and your daddy."

"Why would we do that? I like it here."

"I know you do, but—but Daddy is going to marry Patricia, and I don't think it would be fun to live with her."

Robbie frowned. "Why would he do that?

"Because—because she's pretty," Abby said, uttering the only possible reason she'd found for Nick to marry her.

"You're pretty, Mommy, and you're lots nicer,"

Abby hugged her child. "I'm glad you think so, honey."

"We all think so," Brad told her. "Nick is an idiot if he can't see that."

"Life doesn't stay still, Brad. It's always moving and changing. What you choose one day may not be your choice a year later, because you're in a different place. I guess that's why there are so many divorces." Abby hugged her son to her. At least she hadn't gone through a divorce from Nick. That heartbreak would've been devastating.

Five years ago, she'd thought she could fit in with the Logans. The idea of being part of a big family was exciting. But Nick hadn't given her that option—not because he didn't love her, according to him, but because he wanted to save her.

That heartbreak was bad enough, but divorce meant something different.

She looked at the other two, looking grim as they studied the future. "The time could come when Patricia might be the right choice, even if you don't see it now."

"You're being overly generous, Abby," Kate said. "We're talking Patricia here."

Abby managed to dredge up a smile. "Come on, Kate, it won't be so bad."

"Of course not. She'll treat me like her maid. Just what I wanted, to grow old as the grunt of the family."

"Mom, Nick won't let that happen," Brad assured his mother. "Whatever Nick is, he'd never be mean to you."

"No, but Patricia would. I'm going to start looking for another house to at least rent, if Nick decides to bring Patricia here."

"Will you save a place for me? I don't know how long I can last."

"Of course, dear, you'll always be welcome in any home I have." She paused, looking around the room before she said, "I always thought I would live here until I died."

Abby leaned over and caught Kate's hand. "You never know what kind of excitement life has in store for you. You'll be all right, Kate. You're a smart woman, and you have good sons who will help you. And then there's Mike. Don't forget he promised to save you."

"He did, didn't he?" Kate responded, her face brightening. "Do you think— I wonder what he meant by that remark?"

Abby smiled. "Don't be coy, Kate. I think he's a man you can count on."

"I think so, too." Kate didn't even bother to hide the broad grin.

Nick got in after Abby had gone to bed. After all, she had to get up early in the morning.

His mother was still up, waiting to find out what had happened. She was sitting at the kitchen table nursing a cup of tea.

"What are you doing up, Mom?" Nick asked as he entered the house.

"Nick! Where have you been? What happened?"

"Everything's fine, Mom. It's all over."

"What's over?"

"My engagement to Patricia."

Kate stared at him. "What? Do you mean it?"

"Shh, not so loud. I don't want Abby to find out like this."

Kate stared at him. "But you do intend to tell her, don't you?"

"Well, yes, of course, but I think I owe her some nice memories for our grandchildren."

"Your grandchildren? Oh, my." Kate took a deep breath. "I've been trying to figure out where to move when Patricia moved in! Oh, what a relief! I'm happy for you, too, son. I thought you would be making a horrible mistake if you married Patricia. You'll be safe now, with Abby."

"I don't know that she'll accept. And if she does, I don't want it to be because she wants to make Robbie happy."

Kate stared at Nick. "No wonder you screwed up last time. You don't really know her, do you?"

Nick frowned at her. "What are you talking about?"

"She is the most loving person I've ever met. And honest. She wouldn't accept if she didn't love you. She's already proved she won't depend on you to take care of her. She certainly didn't when she was pregnant and alone."

"I know, but—"

"You've never been pregnant and never will be, but I hope someday you'll go through nine months with a woman who is. It's a scary process, but together you make it. Abby went through the entire nine months alone. She must've been so afraid. But she never took the easy way out."

"I know I owe her for Robbie, for the strength she gave him and the joy she gave him. That must've been harder to come up with than the determination." Nick pulled out a chair at the table.

"Yes, and she hasn't asked for help since she got here, either. That alone ought to be proof that she'll stand on her own."

"I guess so. But I want to do this right. I want to convince her that I love her."

Kate rolled her eyes. "Fine, do it your way. By the way, how did you get Patricia to break off the engagement?"

When Nick told her, Kate exclaimed, "And you expected her to follow those rules? Good heavens! That woman wouldn't even know how to play fair."

"Yeah, well...I have Mike to thank for alerting me. I'd asked him to keep an ear to the ground and he did."

"I'm glad. But I still think you should just tell Abby you love her."

"When? At five-thirty in the morning before she dashes out the door to work? When she's waiting on customers at the café? Or when she's feeding Robbie his snack? Or baking casseroles for dinner? She's one busy lady."

"Yes, she is, but she'll hear about Patricia's behavior when she goes into work."

"Damn! I hadn't thought of that. Now what do I do?"

"I don't know, Nick, but whatever you decide, try putting Abby first this time. I think she deserves that."

Nick never could disagree with his mother.

CHAPTER TWELVE

COFFEE.

That was Abby's first thought when the alarm went off at five-fifteen. It had been a long night, tossing and turning, with Nick the star of her fitful dreams.

Her muscles screamed when she got out of bed, thanks to the backbreaking labor over at the apartment. She worked through the ache and went to the kitchen to put the coffee on. By the time she was dressed, it would be brewed.

She was ready to go back to the kitchen when someone knocked on her bedroom door. Was it Robbie? Was he sick?

Rushing to the door, she swung it open, prepared to take care of her son.

It wasn't Robbie. It was his dad.

"What do you want, Nick?" Abby asked cautiously.

"I need to talk to you."

Abby took about ten seconds to realize she didn't want to talk with Nick in her bedroom. "The coffee should be ready now. Let's go have a cup."

"Okay," he agreed and stood back for her to precede him.

She couldn't imagine what was going on. She usually saw him only at dinnertime each day. Not at five forty-five in the morning. It was too early to deal with the heartache of seeing him and knowing she was leaving.

She poured two cups and Nick carried them to the table.

"I don't have long, Nick," she warned, eager to get away.

"Patricia and I broke up."

He paused but she didn't say anything. The words didn't seem to sink in.

"Unfortunately," Nick continued, "I gave her time to tell people that she chose to break up with me. I told her she had to play fair. But Patricia didn't do what she promised. She went to the café and told everyone I've been sleeping with you while I was engaged to her."

That sunk in. Her eyes widened in shock, but she didn't say anything. She wasn't capable of speaking.

"I wanted to let you know before you went to work. George defended you. I told the man who repeated the rumor that it wasn't true, but I was afraid you'd be upset."

She finally found the words, as anger built inside her. "Yes, I might be upset!"

"Say whatever you want to say, honey. I know it's unfair."

"I don't need you to tell me that! I'm only here because you threatened to take away my child! How could she say such a thing?"

"Calm down, Abby. I stopped it as soon as I could."

Abby shoved back her chair, her coffee untouched. "She'd better stay away from the café, because I have no intention of being nice to her!"

"That's fine with me."

His soothing words only irritated her. "I don't need your approval, Nick Logan!" Then she stomped out of the kitchen.

Nick was still sitting at the table when Kate came into the kitchen at six-fifteen. He wasn't capable of moving. He just sat there, slumped in his chair.

"Are you ready for breakfast already?" she asked in surprise.

He shook his head. "I got up early to talk to Abby."

"Good. So you explained about Patricia? What did she say?"

"She got mad and left. Said she hoped Patricia didn't come to the café because she wouldn't serve her." He turned sad eyes up to his mother. "But she didn't say anything about us."

Kate put a hand on one of his shoulders. "I never thought I'd say this, but you are the dumbest person I've ever seen."

"What?"

She took the seat opposite him. "Well, of course she didn't say anything, Nick. The last time she gave herself to you, you sent her away. She'd be crazy to assume you want her now."

The workings of the female mind alluded him. He could run a ranch and handle the herd, but when it came to Abby, he was a tenderfoot.

He needed advice.

"What do I do now?"

Kate smiled at him. "It's easy. All you have to do is show her you love her. You could ask her to marry you again. That might do it. But," she warned, "I wouldn't sleep with her until you were married. You risked that once, and look what happened."

"I'm not ashamed of Robbie!"

"That's not what I meant. But after what Patricia said, if you have a baby any sooner than nine months, people will take that as proof that Patricia was right."

"Damn. I hadn't thought about that. Okay, so I have to court her in public and keep my hands off her until I've married her." No matter how difficult that would be. And he already knew it would be extremely difficult. He'd waited too long to be together with Abby. And now with his son, too.

He got up from the table.

"Where are you going?" Kate asked. "You haven't had breakfast yet."

"I'm going in to town."

Kate knew exactly where he was going. "Son, are you sure?"

"I'm sure. I'm not going to lose her now."

"Three short stacks with sausage and a Cowboy Special." Abby put down the four plates in front of the foursome that had become breakfast regulars at the café. She gave them each a sunny smile. "Enjoy your meals, gentlemen." As she turned away, the smile died on her lips.

The one customer she hoped not to see was sitting in the front booth.

Nick was watching her, his dark eyes taking in every inch of her. She couldn't help but feel a flush that had nothing to do with the breakfast rush and all to do with the handsome cowboy. It didn't matter. She may be running from him, but she knew she'd never be able to run from the feelings he aroused in her.

But she had to.

Steeling herself, she stepped toward him, standing there with her pencil poised over the order pad.

"What can I get you?"

"I'll take a lifetime with you, Abby."

What he said didn't register at first. She stared at her pad, fumbling with her pencil. Then his words sunk in. But her heart didn't flip at his proposal. Instead she felt a pain stabbing her insides. It was too late for them. Couldn't Nick see that?

Fighting the sting of tears in her eyes, she affected a matter-of-fact tone. "That's not on the menu. Try again."

"Abby—"

She kept her resolve. "Either order or leave. I've got other customers."

"I'll take two eggs over easy, a stack of pancakes, bacon and black coffee."

Quickly she spun around and headed for the kitchen. She needed to get away from Nick before she fell into his arms, sobbing because he wanted her again. But for how long? He'd dumped her the last time life had changed. He might do so again.

In the kitchen, she leaned against the wall and the tears started to fall.

"What's wrong, Abby girl?" George asked.

She wiped the tears and stood up. "N-nothing, George. I—I just needed a minute." She ripped Nick's order off the pad and handed it to him. "Here's the latest order."

"You've got an order up," he told her, still looking at her skeptically. "You sure you're okay?"

"I'm fine," she answered with a fake smile. Then she picked up the two plates and brought them out to table five. Passing Nick, she kept her eyes directly ahead, never looking at him. But she felt his gaze on her.

She probably always would.

Nick remained in his booth, long after he ate his breakfast and nursed two cups of coffee. Abby had stopped coming back for refills.

He was still there when Kate came in to work.

She greeted her son. "What are you still doing here?"

"Waiting to talk to Abby."

Kate sighed. "Son, I've never known you to languish like this. Just do it." She looked around the café, which was still fairly crowded. "I'm not sure forcing the issue in public is a good idea."

"But I have to make her understand."

"I won't say anything. Just remember Abby gets to make her own choices, just as you do."

"That's what scares me," Nick muttered as Abby waltzed past him again.

"See that? She acts like I'm invisible, even after I told her I broke it off with Patricia."

"What makes you think she'll assume you want her? You didn't say anything, did you?"

"Not really. I was afraid," he finally admitted.

"Do you think she wasn't afraid when she found out she was carrying your child? It's your turn to be afraid."

"Yeah, I guess so." Drawing a deep breath, he said, "I'm going back to the ranch. I've got some branding to do. At least that I know how to deal with."

Out of the corner of her eye, Abby watched Nick leave the café. She'd thought perhaps he'd decided about his future and wanted her in it. But apparently she was wrong.

If he'd been seriously interested in her, he wouldn't have left.

But he had.

And now she knew she had no choice but to leave the Logan ranch tonight. She couldn't stay one more night and have to run in to Nick in the kitchen or coming down the hall. It was time to move on.

She told Kate, who didn't take the news too well. Nor did Robbie, when she picked him up from school. But she knew the boy would come around. After all, as she reminded him, they would always be together.

After she got him a snack at the café, she took Robbie up to the apartment and gave him a few chores he could do by himself.

She took on the heavier work, throwing herself into it so she could block out any thoughts of Nick Logan. She only stopped, hours later, when Robbie complained that it had to be dinnertime. His stomach was growling.

When they got back to the ranch, Robbie jumped out

of the car and raced for the house. Abby got out more slowly, whether it was because of the pain in her back or the dread she felt at the possibility of seeing Nick.

As soon as she walked in, Robbie asked her, "Can I go check on Baby?"

She ruffled his hair. "Sure you can." The little boy started running for the door.

"Put on your jacket!" Abby called. Once he had left, she turned to Kate. "I wondered if you'd keep Robbie for me tonight. Then I'll pick him up after school and move his clothes and things over to the apartment. We'll be out of your hair as quickly as possible, that way."

"You know I don't want you out of my hair. Won't you at least stay until the end of the week?"

"I can't, Kate. But I think Robbie will be okay here for tonight. I'm going to go tell him as soon as I pack my bags and put them in the car."

Then she went for the room she'd been calling her own.

Nick had finally developed a plan. A consultation with George had him arriving at the café the minute Abby had left the second-floor apartment.

With the help of one of his mother's handmade quilts, he closed off the last booth from the rest of the café. He spread a linen tablecloth over the Formica top and set it with his mother's best china. Then he put some late-blooming flowers in a vase. The finishing touch was the candles he'd picked up. He spread the glass votives all along the windowsill and down the center of the table.

He stepped back to observe. It was a fine-looking table for two.

"What's going on back there?" he heard someone ask. He poked his head around. "I'm planning a romantic dinner."

"For that Atwell woman?" one of the men asked.

"No, for Abby." The waitresses giggled and Nick smiled at them.

"Good. We like her."

"Me, too," Nick agreed, grinning even more.

In his pocket, he had an even bigger surprise that he'd driven into Pinedale to purchase. Abby wasn't like Patricia, picking the most expensive ring she could find. So he wanted to get Abby a ring that suited her, but showed how much he loved her.

One of the waitresses went to answer the phone. She hung up and said, "Abby just left the ranch. Your mom says she has her bags packed."

"Thanks," Nick said, grateful for all the help. "Watch and see if she goes up the back stairs."

He went to the kitchen to get one of Abby's casseroles, as George had promised. He couldn't think of anything better to serve Abby than her own cooking.

He placed it on the table with some vegetables and hot rolls, then lit the candles. He waited for the waitress to tell him where Abby would go first.

"She's going around back."

Nick moved to the back door and watched as Abby dragged herself up the stairs as if the weight of the world was on her shoulders. He hoped by the end of the evening she'd feel much better.

Once he knew she'd reached the apartment, he slipped out the back door and climbed the stairs after her.

She was sitting on a cot she'd probably bought at the general store, tears running down her cheeks.

"Abby? Are you okay?" he asked softly.

She jerked up. "Wh-what are you doing here?"

"I thought maybe you'd join me for dinner. You haven't eaten, have you?"

"I have a lot to do."

He stepped forward and took her hand. "Come on, Abby. You have to eat or you won't have the strength to keep going. Just come eat with me and then you can come up and work if that's what you want to do."

"I—I look a mess. I don't want anyone to see me."

"I know a special restaurant where no one will see us. I promise. Besides, you look beautiful to me."

"Nick, that's sweet of you, but—"

"Come on. It's not far." He tugged on her hand and got her moving down the stairs.

When they reached the back door of the café, he opened it and escorted her to the booth he'd sectioned off. He couldn't take his eyes off her as he parted the quilt and let her see the candlelit table. She looked so beautiful in the dim light, the fire dancing off her green eyes.

"Why— How—" She took in all the fineries, then looked at him. "It's lovely, Nick. Are those your mother's good dishes?" she asked, suddenly recognizing them.

"Yeah. She loaned them to me."

"You'd better be careful not to damage them. They're very important to her."

"Not as important as you." He leaned in to her, but Abby stepped back.

"Why is the quilt hanging here?" she asked, her voice a bit unsteady.

"I wanted us to dine privately, and this is the only restaurant in town."

"You went to a lot of trouble."

He was glad she noticed. "Yeah. Come sit down. Dinner is on the table."

Abby slid into the booth, and Nick opposite her. He uncovered the casserole once they were settled. "I hope you don't mind," he said, "but I couldn't find better food than yours."

"No, but George might. I made that for dinner tonight."

"He donated it to us. Here, let me serve you." Nick made her plate, then his own. It felt good to serve Abby for a change.

They picked up their forks but Nick couldn't taste what he ate. His focus was on the curious glances Abby kept shooting in his direction.

Finally she put her fork down and said, "All right, Nick, what's going on?"

"What do you mean?" he asked innocently. "I thought a woman should have a nice fancy dinner once in a while. I think the only dinners we had alone were picnics."

"There's nothing wrong with picnics. They're spontaneous and—and fun."

"I agree."

"Then why are we—"

"I'm trying to be romantic, Abby. Don't you want me to be romantic?"

"I—I don't know. What is that you want?"

She'd just opened the barn door. He had to enter—now or never.

Taking a deep breath, he looked into her eyes. "I want you, Abby. I want you to be my wife, to live with me until we die, to make more babies with me. Would you be willing to do that?"

For what seemed an eternity, she didn't say a word. She merely looked at him, and he held his breath. Then she opened her lips and asked, "Why?"

He'd expected her to no, hoped she'd say yes or just throw her arms around his neck and kiss him right on the mouth. He'd never expected her to ask why.

She clarified it for him. "Is it because I'm Robbie's mother, or because I fit in with your family?"

"You have to ask that?"

"Yes, Nick, I do. Last time I believed we'd be together. But you sent me away."

"And that was the worst mistake I've ever made. I thought you'd at least come back to visit. But you never did."

"I couldn't without revealing Robbie. I didn't know what to do. And you never came calling like I believed you would."

She was right. "So we both lived in misery. Or at least I did."

"Until you got engaged to Patricia."

He snickered. "Then the misery got worse. I thought I was doing what my mother wanted. And I ended up making a big mess of everything. But then I found out about you and Robbie, and I started looking for a way out. Finally I just broke up with Patricia. I should've done that the minute I brought you back to town, but I was angry with you."

"Are you mad at me now?"

He reached across the table and caught her hand. "No, Abby, I'm not. I'm in love with you."

Her eyes seemed to glisten then, and he could swear he heard her breath catch.

"I'm so much in love with you I have to fight crawling over the table and making love to you right here."

"Nick, you wouldn't!" she said on a gasp.

He gave her a sexy grin to tease her, but in the end he acquiesced. "Not here. But I will, in our bed, every night when we're married."

"You're sure this time?"

He knew what she was asking. "I was sure last time, Abby. But I thought I had to do the right thing. This time, the right thing is what I want with all my heart."

His hands tightened on hers as he finally said the words he should have said long ago. "So, Abby Stafford, will you marry me and make me the happiest cowboy in Wyoming?"

Abby sent him a sparkling smile through the tears that now streamed down her cheeks. "Yes."

He half rose and leaned over the table to wipe them away with his thumbs. She never looked more beautiful to him and he couldn't believe this incredible woman was finally going to be his. Lowering his head, he sealed their engagement with a soft kiss that, too long denied, quickly heated. Only the burst of applause and cheering that erupted behind the quilt pulled them up short.

"I guess our private dining wasn't so private after all," Nick said with a smile against her lips. "But it was the best I could manage."

"I think we could have started a tradition in Sydney Creek. 'George's Private Dining.'" Abby smiled at him. "We could push back the quilt and celebrate with them."

"Not yet."

"Do we have something else to discuss?"

"Yeah. This." He swooped down and kissed her again with all he had. After all, it had to last till their wedding.

They were married the next week.

Neither of them wanted to put it off any longer. After all, they'd already waited five long years.

When Abby walked down the aisle, wearing her diamond ring that Nick had given her in their private dining room, she was accompanied by her son. Robbie proudly bore her arm and led her to his beaming father. Kate was the matron of Honor, and Mike Dunleavy was Nick's best man. Nick decided that would please his mother, who constantly smiled at anything and everything these days. His four brothers were the ushers and Julie organized the reception.

The whole town of Sydney Creek attended.

Another couple had already used the private dining facilities at the café, and Abby suspected Kate would never get her quilt back. It would become a Sydney Creek tradition.

Abby looked up at her new husband as he twirled her

around the dance floor. "Five years ago, I wouldn't have believed we'd have a happy ending," she whispered to him so the other dancers wouldn't hear.

"I wouldn't have believed it two weeks ago," Nick returned.

She let her eyes feast on him. "This day is everything I've ever wanted, Nick. Thanks."

His eyes darkened. "Just wait until tonight. It'll only get better." Then he began to nuzzle her neck, raining a trail of soft, light kisses on her neck.

"Nick, everyone's watching!"

"So let them watch. I'm kissing my wife."

He swooped down and kissed her on the mouth, dipping her backward in an exaggerated flourish.

Robbie laughed and clapped his hands.

And the whole town cheered.

* * * * *

Award-winning author Stevi Mittman delivers
another hysterical mystery, featuring Teddi Bayer,
an irrepressible heroine, and her to-die-for hero,
Detective Drew Scoones. After all, life on Long
Island can be murder!

*Turn the page for a sneak peek
at the warm and funny fourth book,
WHOSE NUMBER IS UP, ANYWAY?,
in the Teddi Bayer series,
by STEVI MITTMAN.
On sale August 7*

CHAPTER 1

"Before redecorating a room, I always advise my clients to empty it of everything but one chair. Then I suggest they move that chair from place to place, sitting in it, until the placement feels right. Trust your instincts when deciding on furniture placement. Your room should "feel right."

—TipsFromTeddi.com

Gut feelings. You know, that gnawing in the pit of your stomach that warns you that you are about to do the absolute stupidest thing you could do? Something that will ruin life as you know it?

I've got one now, standing at the butcher counter in King Kullen, the grocery store in the same strip mall as L.I. Lanes, the bowling alley cum billiard parlor I'm in the process of redecorating for its "Grand Opening."

I realize being in the wrong supermarket probably doesn't sound exactly dire to you, but you aren't the one buying your father a brisket at a store your mother will somehow know isn't Waldbaum's.

And then, June Bayer isn't your mother.

The woman behind the counter has agreed to go into the freezer to find a brisket for me, since there aren't any in the case. There are packages of pork tenderloin, piles of spare ribs and rolls of sausage, but no briskets.

Warning Number Two, right? I should be so out of here.

But no, I'm still in the same spot when she comes back out, brisketless, her face ashen. She opens her mouth as if she is going to scream, but only a gurgle comes out.

And then she pinballs out from behind the counter, knocking bottles of Peter Luger Steak Sauce to the floor on her way, now hitting the tower of cans at the end of the prepared foods aisle and sending them sprawling, now making her way down the aisle, careening from side to side as she goes.

Finally, from a distance, I hear her shout, "He's deeeeeeaaaad! Joey's deeeeeaaaad."

My first thought is *You should always trust your gut.*

My second thought is that now, somehow, my mother will know I was in King Kullen. For weeks I will have to hear "What did you expect?" as though whenever you go to King Kullen someone turns up dead. And if the detective investigating the case turns out to be Detective Drew Scoones . . .well, I'll never hear the end of that from her, either.

She still suspects I murdered the guy who was found dead on my doorstep last Halloween just to get Drew back into my life.

Several people head for the butcher's freezer and I position myself to block them. If there's one thing I've learned from finding people dead—and the guy on my doorstep wasn't the first one—it's that the police get very testy when you mess with their murder scenes.

"You can't go in there until the police get here," I say, stationing myself at the end of the butcher's counter and in front of the Employees Only door, acting as if I'm some sort of authority. "You'll contaminate the evidence if it turns out to be murder."

Shouts and chaos. You'd think I'd know better than to throw the word *murder* around. Cell phones are flipping open and tongues are wagging.

I amend my statement quickly. "Which, of course, it probably isn't. Murder, I mean. People die all the time, and it's not always in hospitals or their own beds, or..." I babble when I'm nervous, and the idea of someone dead on the other side of the freezer door makes me very nervous.

So does the idea of seeing Drew Scoones again. Drew and I have this on-again, off-again sort of thing... that I kind of turned off.

Who knew he'd take it so personally when he tried to get serious and I responded by saying we could talk about *us* tomorrow—and then caught a plane to my parents' condo in Boca the next day? In July. In the middle of a job.

For some crazy reason, he took that to mean that I was avoiding him and the subject of *us*.

That was three months ago. I haven't seen him since.

The manager, who identifies himself and points to his nameplate in case I don't believe him, says he has to go into *his cooler*. "Maybe Joey's not dead," he says.

"Maybe he can be saved, and you're letting him die in there. Did you ever think of that?"

In fact, I hadn't. But I had thought that the murderer might try to go back in to make sure his tracks were covered, so I say that I will go in and check.

Which means that the manager and I couple up and go in together while everyone pushes against the doorway to peer in, erasing any chance of finding clean prints on that Employee Only door.

I expect to find carcasses of dead animals hanging from hooks, and maybe Joey hanging from one, too. I think it's going to be very creepy and I steel myself, only to find a rather benign series of shelves with large slabs of meat laid out carefully on them, along with boxes and boxes marked simply Chicken.

Nothing scary here, unless you count the body of a middle-aged man with graying hair sprawled faceup on the floor. His eyes are wide open and unblinking. His shirt is stiff. His pants are stiff. His body is stiff. And his expression, you should forgive the pun—is frozen. Bill-the-manager crosses himself and stands mute while I pronounce the guy dead in a sort of *happy now?* tone.

"We should not be in here," I say, and he nods his head emphatically and helps me push people out of the doorway just in time to hear the police sirens and see the cop cars pull up outside the big store windows.

Bobbie Lyons, my partner in Teddi Bayer Interior Designs (and also my neighbor, my best friend and my private fashion police), and Mark, our carpenter (and my dogsitter, confidant, and ego booster), rush in from next door. They beat the cops by a half step and shout out my name. People point in my direction.

After all the publicity that followed the unfortunate incident during which I shot my ex-husband, Rio Gallo, and then the subsequent murder of my first client—which I solved, I might add—it seems like the whole world, or at least all of Long Island, knows who I am.

Mark asks if I'm all right. (Did I remember to mention that the man is drop-dead-gorgeous-but-a-decade-too-young-for-me-yet-too-old-for-my-daughter-thank-god?) I don't get a chance to answer him because the police are quickly closing in on the store manager and me.

"The woman—" I begin telling the police. Then I have to pause for the manager to fill in her name, which he does: *Fran.*

I continue. "Right. Fran. Fran went into the freezer to get a brisket. A moment later she came out and screamed that Joey was dead. So I'd say she was the one who discovered the body."

"And you are…?" the cop asks me. It comes out a bit like who do I *think* I am, rather than who am I really?

"An innocent bystander," Bobbie, hair perfect, makeup just right, says, carefully placing her body between the cop and me.

"And she was just leaving," Mark adds. They each take one of my arms.

Fran comes into the inner circle surrounding the cops. In case it isn't obvious from the hairnet and blood-stained white apron with Fran embroidered on it, I explain that she was the butcher who was going for the brisket. Mark and Bobbie take that as a signal that I've done my job and they can now get me out of there. They twist around, with me in the middle, as if we're a Rockettes line, until we are facing away from the butcher counter. They've managed to propel me a few steps toward the exit when disaster—in the form of a Mazda RX7 pulling up at the loading curb—strikes.

Mark's grip on my arm tightens like a vise. "Too late," he says.

Bobbie's expletive is unprintable. "Maybe there's a back door," she suggests, but Mark is right. It's too late.

I've laid my eyes on Detective Scoones. And while my gut is trying to warn me that my heart shouldn't go there, regions farther south are melting at just the sight of him.

"Walk," Bobbie orders me.

And I try to. Really.

Walk, I tell my feet. *Just put one foot in front of the other.*

I can do this because I know, in my heart of hearts, that if Drew Scoones was still interested in me, he'd have gotten in touch with me after I returned from Boca. And he didn't.

Since he's a detective, Drew doesn't have to wear one of those dark blue Nassau County Police uniforms. Instead, he's got on jeans, a tight-fitting T-shirt and a tweedy sports jacket. If you think that sounds good, you should see him. Chiseled features, cleft chin, brown hair that's naturally a little sandy in the front, a smile that…well, that doesn't matter. He isn't smiling now.

He walks up to me, tucks his sunglasses into his breast pocket and looks me over from head to toe.

"Well, if it isn't Miss Cut and Run," he says. "Aren't you supposed to be somewhere in Florida or something?" He looks at Mark accusingly, as if he was covering for me when he told Drew I was gone.

"Detective Scoones?" one of the uniforms says. "The stiff's in the cooler and the woman who found him is over there." He jerks his head in Fran's direction.

Drew continues to stare at me.

You know how when you were young, your mother always told you to wear clean underwear in case you were in an accident? And how, a little farther on, she told you not to go out in hair rollers because you never knew who you might see—or who might see you? And how now your best friend says she wouldn't be caught dead without makeup and suggests you shouldn't either?

Okay, today, *finally,* in my overalls and Converse sneakers, I get it.

I brush my hair out of my eyes. "Well, I'm back," I say. As if he hasn't known my exact whereabouts. The man is a detective, for heaven's sake. "Been back awhile."

Bobbie has watched the exchange and apparently decided she's given Drew all the time he deserves. "And we've got work to do, so…" she says, grabbing my arm and giving Drew a little two-fingered wave goodbye.

As I back up a foot or two, the store manager sees his chance and places himself in front of Drew, trying to get his attention. Maybe what makes Drew such a good detective is his ability to focus.

Only what he's focusing on is me.

"Phone broken? Carrier pigeon died?" he asks me,

taking in Fran, the manager, the meat counter and that Employees Only door, all without taking his eyes off me.

Mark tries to break the spell. "We've got work to do there, you've got work to do here, Scoones," Mark says to him, gesturing toward next door. "So it's back to the alley for us."

Drew's lip twitches. "You working the alley now?" he says.

"If you'd like to follow me," Bill-the-manager, clearly exasperated, says to Drew—who doesn't respond. It's as if waiting for my answer is all he has to do.

So, fine. "You knew I was back," I say.

The man has known my whereabouts every hour of the day for as long as I've known him. And my mother's not the only one who won't buy that he "just happened" to answer this particular call. In fact, I'm willing to bet my children's lunch money that he's taken every call within ten miles of my home since the day I got back.

And now he's gotten lucky.

"*You* could have called *me*," I say.

"You're the one who said *tomorrow* for our talk and then flew the coop, chickie," he says. "I figured the ball was in your court."

"Detective?" the uniform says. "There's something you ought to see in here."

Drew gives me a look that amounts to *in or out?*

He could be talking about the investigation, or about our relationship.

Bobbie tries to steer me away. Mark's fists are balled.

Drew waits me out, knowing I won't be able to resist what might be a murder investigation.

Finally he turns and heads for the cooler.

And, like a puppy dog, I follow.

Bobbie grabs the back of my shirt and pulls me to a halt.

"I'm just going to show him something," I say, yanking away.

"Yeah," Bobbie says, pointedly looking at the buttons on my blouse. The two at breast level have popped. "That's what I'm afraid of."

REASONS FOR REVENGE

A brand-new provocative miniseries by *USA TODAY*
bestselling author **Maureen Child** begins with

SCORNED
BY THE BOSS

Jefferson Lyon is a man used to having his own way.
He runs his shipping empire from California, and
his admin Caitlyn Monroe runs the rest of his world.
When Caitlin decides she's had enough and needs
new scenery, Jefferson devises a plan to get her back.
Jefferson *never* loses, but little does he know that
he's in a competition....

Don't miss any of the other titles from the
REASONS FOR REVENGE trilogy by
USA TODAY bestselling author **Maureen Child.**

SCORNED BY THE BOSS #1816
Available August 2007

SEDUCED BY THE RICH MAN #1820
Available September 2007

CAPTURED BY THE BILLIONAIRE #1826
Available October 2007

Only from Silhouette Desire!

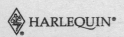

HARLEQUIN®

American ROMANCE®

TEXAS LEGACIES: THE CARRIGANS

Get to the Heart of a Texas Family

WITH

THE RANCHER NEXT DOOR
by
Cathy Gillen Thacker

She'll Run The Ranch—And Her Life—Her Way!

On her alpaca ranch in Texas, Rebecca encounters
constant interference from Trevor McCabe, the
bossy rancher next door. Rebecca becomes very
friendly with Vince Owen, her other neighbor and
Trevor's archrival from college. Trevor's problem
is convincing Rebecca that he is on her side, and
aware of Vince's ulterior motives. But Trevor has
fallen for her in the process....

On sale July 2007

REQUEST YOUR FREE BOOKS!
2 FREE NOVELS PLUS 2
FREE GIFTS!

HARLEQUIN ROMANCE®

From the Heart, For the Heart

YES! Please send me 2 FREE Harlequin Romance® novels and my 2 FREE gifts. After receiving them, if I don't wish to receive any more books, I can return the shipping statement marked "cancel." If I don't cancel, I will receive 4 brand-new novels every month and be billed just $3.57 per book in the U.S., or $4.05 per book in Canada, plus 25¢ shipping and handling per book and applicable taxes, if any*. That's a savings of over 15% off the cover price! I understand that accepting the 2 free books and gifts places me under no obligation to buy anything. I can always return a shipment and cancel at any time. Even if I never buy another book from Harlequin, the two free books and gifts are mine to keep forever.

114 HDN EEV7 314 HDN EEWK

Name	(PLEASE PRINT)	
Address		Apt.
City	State/Prov.	Zip/Postal Code

Signature (if under 18, a parent or guardian must sign)

Mail to the **Harlequin Reader Service®:**
IN U.S.A.: P.O. Box 1867, Buffalo, NY 14240-1867
IN CANADA: P.O. Box 609, Fort Erie, Ontario L2A 5X3

Not valid to current Harlequin Romance subscribers.

Want to try two free books from another line?
Call 1-800-873-8635 or visit www.morefreebooks.com.

* Terms and prices subject to change without notice. NY residents add applicable sales tax. Canadian residents will be charged applicable provincial taxes and GST. This offer is limited to one order per household. All orders subject to approval. Credit or debit balances in a customer's account(s) may be offset by any other outstanding balance owed by or to the customer. Please allow 4 to 6 weeks for delivery.

Your Privacy: Harlequin is committed to protecting your privacy. Our Privacy Policy is available online at www.eHarlequin.com or upon request from the Reader Service. From time to time we make our lists of customers available to reputable firms who may have a product or service of interest to you. If you would prefer we not share your name and address, please check here. ☐

HR07

Coming Next Month

#3967 MARRYING HER BILLIONAIRE BOSS Myrna Mackenzie
Black sheep Carson Banick needs a wife to save his family's fortune.
Beth Crayton, Carson's feisty PA, is determined to succeed on her own,
without a man. As the attraction between them grows, Carson must decide
what's more important: saving his family, or claiming Beth's heart?

#3968 THE ITALIAN'S WIFE BY SUNSET Lucy Gordon
The Rinucci Brothers
Sensible Della Hadley should have known better than to embark on an affair
with irresistible playboy Carlo Rinucci. She knows such passion cannot last,
despite Carlo's protests that their love is forever. Can Carlo make Della his
bride before the sun sets on their affair?

#3969 HIS MIRACLE BRIDE Marion Lennox
Castle at Dolphin Bay
Shanni Jefferson doesn't do family! But when she finds herself a live-in
nanny to five little children—and working side by side with their gorgeous
guardian Pierce MacLaughlin—she begins to wonder whether family life with
this adorable brood might suit her after all.

#3970 REUNITED: MARRIAGE IN A MILLION Liz Fielding
Secrets We Keep
Popular TV presenter Belle is married to gorgeous billionaire Ivo, and lives in
a beautiful mansion. Yet beneath the veneer of her perfect life is the truth of
their marriage of convenience. But Belle is deeply in love with Ivo, and only
wishes for a baby to make their family whole.

#3971 BABY TWINS: PARENTS NEEDED Teresa Carpenter
Baby on Board
Rachel Adams's independent life is turned upside down when she's named
guardian to two orphaned twins! Then gorgeous co-guardian Ford Sullivan
turns up. Being this close to Ford makes Rachel wonder whether stand-in
mom and dad could become forever bride and groom?

#3972 BREAK UP TO MAKE UP Fiona Harper
Nick and Adele Hughes's marriage is over. But, stranded in a picturesque
cottage, they find they cannot resist the spark that has always fizzed
between them. As the twinkling firelight works its magic, Nick and Adele
discover that the wonderful thing about breaking up is making up.

HRCNM0707